Praise for

Girl's Best Friend

"A barking good mystery." —*Discovery Girls*

"*Girl's Best Friend* clips the reader onto a touching, funny story-leash that twists and turns; dogs, their humans, twins of all ages, old friends, and even apartments are not what they seem at first. At least, not always . . . Margolis leaves you wanting to look twice at every familiar gesture and setting."
—Blue Balliett, author of *Chasing Vermeer*

"Maggie Brooklyn is a smart, funny, capable detective, and a *real kid*. Sequel, please."
—Adam Rex, author of *The True Meaning of Smekday*

"What better cover for a detective than a neighborhood dog walker? Leslie Margolis has found the perfect mix—a city story, a tween story, *and* a mystery that truly keeps you guessing."
—Gordon Korman, author of
The 39 Clues: The Emperor's Code and *Framed*

"Maggie is a friendly and thoughtful narrator with a sharply logical mind; readers . . . will appreciate her intellect and bravery, and applaud her success." —*Publishers Weekly*

"While the well-crafted mysteries are foremost, it's the relatable, witty protagonist that makes this novel stand out. . . . When this dog walker turned detective returns, she'll be welcome." —*Horn Book*

"This is the kind of good, solid mystery that slides neatly into a weekend or summer evening." —*BCCB*

Books by Leslie Margolis

THE MAGGIE BROOKLYN MYSTERIES
Girl's Best Friend
Vanishing Acts

◆ ◆ ◆

THE ANNABELLE UNLEASHED series
Boys Are Dogs
Girls Acting Catty
Everybody Bugs Out

a maggie brooklyn mystery

Girl's Best Friend

Leslie Margolis

BLOOMSBURY

NEW YORK BERLIN LONDON SYDNEY

For Leo

First published in the United States of America in October 2010
by Bloomsbury Books for Young Readers
Paperback edition published in October 2011
www.bloomsburykids.com

For information about permission to reproduce selections from this book, write to
Permissions, Bloomsbury BFYR, 175 Fifth Avenue, New York, New York 10010

The Library of Congress has cataloged the hardcover edition as follows:
Margolis, Leslie.
Girl's best friend / by Leslie Margolis. —1st U.S. ed.
p.   cm.   — (A Maggie Brooklyn mystery)
Summary: In Brooklyn, New York, twelve-year-old dog-walker Maggie, aided by her twin
brother Finn and best friend Lucy, investigates someone she believes is stealing pets.
ISBN 978-1-59990-525-9 (hardcover)
[1. Dog walking—Fiction. 2. Junior high schools—Fiction. 3. Schools—Fiction.
4. Brothers and sisters—Fiction. 5. Twins—Fiction. 6. Family life—New York (State)—
Brooklyn—Fiction. 7. Brooklyn (New York, N.Y.)—Fiction. 8. Mystery and detective
stories.] I. Title.
PZ7.M33568Gio 2010   [Fic]—dc22   2010000562

ISBN 978-1-59990-690-4 (paperback)

Book design by Nicole Gastonguay
Typeset by Westchester Book Composition
Printed in the U.S.A. by Quad/Graphics, Fairfield, Pennsylvania
3 5 7 9 10 8 6 4 2

All papers used by Bloomsbury Publishing, Inc., are natural, recyclable products
made from wood grown in well-managed forests. The manufacturing processes
conform to the environmental regulations of the country of origin.

Try to be one of the people on whom nothing is lost!
—Henry James

Prologue

· · ·

Mitsy wasn't his, but he wished she were. The dog was his favorite thing about his dad's new girlfriend. Something about the way she carried herself—chin up, tongue out, black fur mussed, puny but determined— warmed his heart.

If only he hadn't offered to walk her that scorching hot Saturday in July. He'd do anything for the chance to go back. Change one tiny detail—the weather, his thirst, even the time of day—and things might've been different.

These thoughts kept him up at night. Tortured him. But the facts remained: It was hot. He got thirsty and ducked into a deli for a drink.

The owner balked and pointed to the sign, which read TWO-LEGGED CREATURES ONLY.

So he led Mitsy to the sidewalk and triple-knot tied her to a parking meter.

"I'll be back in a few seconds," he promised, not realizing that a few seconds were all it would take.

The problem was too many choices: Black cherry or cream soda? Lemonade or lime? Strawberry flavored or mango? Sparkling or flat?

Nothing stood out.

When he checked on Mitsy she stared right back at him, dark eyes anxious. Like she smelled something dangerous.

So he grabbed an iced tea, plain and simple. Headed for the cash register. Paid. Stepped back outside and gasped.

Mitsy's leash still dangled from the meter, the knot tied tight.

But Mitsy? She was gone.

Chapter 1

* * *

I am going to talk to Milo Sanchez today.

Today I'm going to talk to Milo.

I must talk to him.

Now.

Okay, now-ish.

Unless I wait until tomorrow. Maybe today I should just buy a slice of pizza and head home.

No, that would be insane. No one comes to the Pizza Den for the pizza. Their crust is way soggy and the service stinks. When you order a slice of pepperoni, there's a very good chance you'll get sausage instead. Its atmosphere is even worse. The place is so dark and musty, they should change their name to Animal Den.

Still, practically every seventh grader at Fiske Street Junior High hangs out at the Pizza Den after school because that's where everyone goes. It's where things happen. And I had just realized something.

There are people who make things happen, people to whom things happen, and then there's everyone else: those who hang around and watch. I've been watching for too long and that's got to change—now.

Well, soon.

I glanced across the room at Milo, leaning against the post that holds up the sagging ceiling in the corner. Arms crossed, head tilted, dark hair falling over his big brown eyes, Milo leans better than any boy I know. He's probably the best leaner in all of Brooklyn, or at least in Park Slope, which is the neighborhood where we live.

He could win a gold medal for it. Nike would offer him sponsorship if they knew, but Milo would refuse because he's not a sellout. I don't think so, anyway. I don't know him all that well.

Okay, fine—we haven't actually spoken. Except for once, last month when I followed him too closely and accidentally stepped on the heel of his left sneaker and it came off and he stumbled and turned around to look at me. Not annoyed, like he thought I'd done it on purpose. More like confused, and I said, "Sorry," and he said, " 'sokay." And he smiled.

I think. It's entirely possible that I imagined the smile part. It happened so long ago I can't be certain, but none of that matters. All that counts is now—this very moment—because we're about to have a real conversation.

We have to, because the hole in his navy blue sweater is huge. I sit behind Milo in science, and three weeks ago his sweater looked almost new, with just one loose thread at the seam near his shoulder. But then he pulled at it during Mrs. Gander's lecture on isotopes and it ripped. That rip turned into a hole and I've watched it grow every single day. Inch by inch, or, as Madame Curie would say (before she died of radiation poisoning), centimeter by centimeter. I promised myself I'd talk to Milo before his sweater unraveled completely.

I just couldn't figure out what to say.

What's the homework in science? Too obvious.

Congrats on winning the all-school speed chess match? Too nerdy.

I saw you heading into Southpaw last Saturday with a guitar strapped to your back. Are you in a band? Too stalkery. I don't want him to think I followed him, because I didn't. I only went three blocks out of my way, in the pouring rain, because I felt like taking a walk that day. It's not pathetic because I had an umbrella.

Nothing seemed right, but then last night it finally came to me: the perfect in. So simple it's brilliant.

I walked over, fast, before I could wimp out.

"Hey, guess what? I walk a dog named Milo." There, I said it. Blurted it out, if you want to get technical. "He's a puggle, which is a cross between a pug and a beagle."

Milo didn't respond.

He didn't even look up.

"He's got that smushed-in pug face but a thinner body and longer legs," I went on, stupidly, as if there were nothing more captivating than this new hybrid dog breed.

Milo said nothing.

Then he went on to say nothing some more.

As a cold panic spread through me, I wondered if maybe I should run. Or hide. Or act like I was talking to the person behind him. Except there was no person behind him—only the grease-stained wall. Could I pretend like I was talking to myself? No, that would be worse.

I began to turn away when Milo raised his head and scrunched his eyebrows together.

I stopped and smiled what I hoped was a tiny and extremely casual smile.

A smile that told him I didn't care one way or the other if he replied.

A smile that didn't hint at the fact that I'd been having pretend conversations with him in my head all week—and that not one of them sounded anything like this.

Suddenly he moved—raised one hand to his ear and tugged out an earbud.

Milo had been listening to his iPod. He wasn't ignoring me. He just didn't hear.

I let out my breath, not realizing I'd been holding it, and waited.

So did Milo.

Oh, right. Now I had to start all over again.

I paused so he could take out his second earbud, but he didn't. Which got me thinking—why only one? Does he think whatever I'm about to say isn't important enough for both ears?

I tried not to take it personally.

"I walk a puggle named Milo." I spoke louder this time, since I had to compete with his music.

"Um, what?" Milo tilted his head.

Progress.

True, Milo had no idea what I was talking about, but at least he acknowledged me. And he didn't seem horrified or anything. He squinted a friendly sort of squint. Like he was smiling with his eyes.

Big beautiful brown eyes—the kind that, gazing into them, made my stomach flip over like a half-cooked pancake.

"I walk this—"

"Um, Maggie." Someone interrupted me. "You don't have a dog."

I cringed. The way she said it—all accusing, like

my *not* having a dog was some horrible offense—
told me, without a doubt, that my least favorite person
heard everything.

And in case I needed the confirmation, Milo looked
over my shoulder and said, "Hey, Ivy."

So I had no choice but to turn around and face her:
Ivy Jeffries. She's got shiny dark hair that's parted in
the middle, falls just below her ears, and always stays
in place. No bangs. Her big blue eyes, dusting of freck-
les across her nose, and tendency to wear pastels make
her seem sweet and innocent, but I know the truth. I
know because she used to be my best friend.

"I never said I had a dog," I told her, standing up
straighter. "I said I walk dogs. It's my after-school job."
I still felt cool, since not a lot of kids I know have jobs,
and mine is a good one. Much better than babysitting.
That's what every other seventh grader who works does,
unless you count Lucy, who knits hats to sell on Etsy—
but I don't because her only client is her grandmother.

Ivy pressed her lips together like that was the only
way to keep from cracking up, but I knew it was just
an act.

"You're a dog walker?" she asked, as if it were
absurd, and burst out laughing.

So did Eve and Katie, her current best friends.

Not that I was about to let them get to me. "Yes, I'm a
dog walker. So what?"

Ivy raised her voice so everyone in the Pizza Den could hear. Probably people outside, too. "So you, like, follow random dogs around and pick up their poop? That's worse than being a garbage collector. You're, like, a janitor to dogs."

"Maggie Brooklyn Sinclair, Dog Janitor," Eve said in this low, official-sounding voice, which made the three of them crack up all over again.

The thing is, I never thought about my job in those terms. I clean up after dogs because it's common courtesy and because it's the law. Break it and you get fined $250—at least in New York City. But picking up after dogs is a very small part of what I do.

Really, my job is about giving animals fresh air and exercise. And I love it.

Dogs are awesome and you always know where you stand with them. Dogs don't suddenly ditch you for no reason, then trash-talk you behind your back—things Ivy would understand all too well. But before I could point this out, she went off.

"Seriously, Maggs? I hope you wash your hands really well after. Because animals carry all kinds of icky diseases." She shuddered an exaggerated—and completely fake—shudder. As if she hadn't been cleaning up after her own dog, Kermit, for years!

Too flustered to point this out, and too humiliated to even look at Milo, I spun around and ran for the door.

Once outside, I turned the corner fast and smacked right into someone.

Pink paper flew through the air, then fluttered to my feet.

"I'm so sorry!" I said.

The woman I'd hit seemed stunned—dark eyes wide behind big glasses. Her red hair was pulled into a tight ponytail. She wore a narrow gray suit and spiky black heels so high they looked hard to walk in.

"Here, let me help." I bent down and she did, too.

And that's when I heard her purse whimper.

I stared at it, puzzled.

It was black and bulky and there it went again—three squeaks. Like she had something alive inside.

Alive and wanting out.

The woman slowly raised her gaze—as if checking to see if I'd noticed.

"Um . . . Is there something—"

"No," she snapped, and she stood up fast. Then she snatched the remaining pages, shouldered her bag, and took off, walking as fast as she could without actually running away.

Chapter 2

. . .

When I'm working, I'm all business: Enter apartment. Greet dog. Put on leash. Exit apartment. Lock door. Walk dog. Return dog. Write note. Lock door. Head to the next apartment and repeat from the beginning.

I'm all about efficiency because I need to be. I only have a two-hour window between when school gets out and when I'm expected home.

That's why I didn't follow the red-haired woman. That, and because she wasn't doing anything wrong, exactly.

Yes, she appeared to be carrying a small animal in her bag. Strange? Of course. Cruel? I think so. But a crime? Not really. It didn't even seem suspicious once I read one of the flyers she'd left behind.

BOUTIQUE BREEDS BY BRENDA was printed in block letters across the top. Below it were sketches of some fancy-looking dogs, then a phone number.

The flyer explained everything. Brenda was a dog breeder and obviously she had a puppy in her purse. I just hoped she wasn't planning on keeping it in there for long—and that her bag had some air holes.

Tossing the flyer into the trash, I headed to work.

Five minutes later I knocked, yelled "Hello!" and let myself into Isabel Rose Franini's apartment.

Isabel was home and on her couch as usual. Her leg was propped up on two red velvet pillows and her crutches lay beside her. Isabel tore something in her knee while salsa dancing last summer. She'd had surgery soon after and still couldn't get around very well, which made taking care of her enormous Irish wolfhound extra hard.

"Maggie, is that you?" she called.

It's pretty much always me, but I'd never say so. "Hi, Isabel. What's new?" I asked as I scratched her dog, Preston, behind the ears. His black and tan fur shined like he'd just been brushed.

"I've lost my glasses and my favorite ring," Isabel said. "The ring's got diamonds and sapphires and emeralds the size of grapes. Loads of sentimental value, too. It was given to me by my first husband, Henry. Or was it my third husband, John? Yes, John. The one who left me for his yoga instructor. I never could trust that man, but his taste in jewelry was divine!"

Isabel is what my dad calls "eccentric." My twin

brother, Finn, thinks she's crazy, and my mom says she's lonely. I know the truth—she's simply Isabel, and there's no point in trying to sum her up in one word because it can't be done. Loud in every way possible, from her voice to her clothes to her purple-and-silver-streaked hair to the way she moves— amplified like she's onstage and performing for the back row. Something she's used to from so many years of singing and dancing on Broadway. She's also warm and funny (both intentionally and not) and scatterbrained and grand and old. Just how old no one knows, because she's been calling herself fifty for at least ten years.

But there's one thing we cannot dispute about Isabel: she's our landlady. We live in her big old brownstone, which is a row house built with large bricks made out of sandstone. Brooklyn is full of them. From the outside, brownstones look like tall single-family townhouses, but actually lots of them are broken up into different apartments. Ours is four stories high, with a wide set of steps leading up to the front door. It contains four separate apartments and my family lives in the one on top.

"Which pair did you lose?" I asked. "Bifocals or distance?"

"Bifocals."

"You're wearing them," I informed her.

She waved her magazine at me—one of my mom's old issues of *O* that she'd probably snagged from the recycling bin out back. "If I'm wearing my glasses, then how come this is all blurry?"

"I mean, you're wearing them on your head."

"Oh dear." Isabel plucked her glasses from her puffed-up do and frowned. "It's the ring that I really need, though. It's quite valuable."

"When did you last see it?"

"Yesterday morning, when I was in the middle of hiding my jewelry."

I nodded.

Isabel hides her jewelry at least once a week. Even the costume stuff. She's convinced that everyone in town is desperate for her old brooches and hundred-year-old engagement rings. And also that they'll find a way to break into her apartment because it's on the ground floor—even though she's got steel bars on the windows and four locks on the door and a dog the size of a small horse. And it's not like our neighborhood is dangerous.

I glanced around her cluttered living room, taking in the mess of old feathered boas and stacks of yellowed newspaper clippings—reviews from her old shows, probably. Her bookshelves could use a good dusting and one of the glass panes of her Tiffany lamp was cracked, but nothing looked out of place.

"The rest of your jewelry is where it's supposed to be?" I asked.

"Every single strand of pearls and opal-studded cuff link is accounted for."

"So tell me what happened." I sat down in the faded yellow armchair, shifting my weight to avoid the broken spring. Preston licked my elbow. I scratched him behind his ears and whispered that we'd leave in a minute. (I don't talk to all my dog clients, but Preston is super smart and I have this sneaking suspicion that he actually understands me.)

"Well, as I mentioned, I was changing hiding places when I was seized with hunger. And you know how I get when I have to eat. So I put everything on the kitchen counter and made myself a peanut butter and banana sandwich, which some people—"

I stood up and coughed. "On second thought, I don't want to keep Preston waiting." I didn't mean to be rude, but if I'm not careful, I could get stuck at Isabel's for hours. "I'll help you look after our walk," I promised.

Isabel smiled. "You know, of course, that twenty years ago I'd have just picked up a new one. I used to buy jewelry the way you kids buy gumdrops."

"I can't remember the last time I bought a gumdrop," I replied as I put on Preston's diamond-studded leash. (Fake stones, I hoped.) "Oh wait. Maybe it was the Friday before never."

"Very funny. My point is, if Henry knew how far I've fallen, he'd be heartbroken."

Isabel says stuff like this constantly. She claims that she and her first husband, Henry, "lived in style," which means they had this big old brownstone all to themselves and threw grand parties every weekend. But that was a long time ago. Henry died young. A truck hit him while he was bicycling down Union Street. A few years later, Isabel married a composer named Salvatore. But he left Isabel for a dancer, which she didn't mind because by then she'd fallen in love with John, a chef at some fancy French restaurant on Smith Street. But then John took up yoga and that was the end of that.

Although Isabel loses stuff all the time—glasses, jewelry, cell phones, husbands—she's managed to hang on to her brownstone for years, but just barely. When John left, he borrowed a lot of money from Isabel, and when I say borrowed, I actually mean stole. By then, Isabel's Broadway career was over. She had nothing left but her house, so she carved it up into apartments and rented them out one by one.

Ours was the first. My parents moved in as soon as they found out they were having me and Finn. Before that they lived in Manhattan, which is just over the bridge but is too expensive for twins. That's why Brooklyn is my middle name, and Finn's as well. It's a running joke between my parents. Had twins, had to move to Brooklyn. I guess it's funny to them.

"I used to get lost in this house," Isabel said, like she could read my mind. "And now I'm crammed into the first floor."

"It's a nice place," I said as I opened the door. "See you later."

"Ciao, bella." Isabel knows about ten words in Italian and uses them whenever possible.

Once outside, I blinked in the afternoon sun. Our brownstone is on Garfield Place, just half a block away from Prospect Park, and that's where I took Preston. It was a bright and crisp apple-crunching sort of day, perfect for strolling through the park with a really cool dog.

And if you're my brother, it was the perfect day for kicking around a soccer ball, which is what he was doing with his best friends, Otto and Red. It's kind of funny that I ran into them since the park stretches on for miles and it's got rolling hills, winding paths, a wooded nature trail, and plenty of places to get lost. Then again, they were playing on the Long Meadow pretty close to the nearest park entrance, so it wasn't that crazy.

Anyway, I waved, and once Finn noticed me he called a time-out and jogged over. Otto and Red ignored me, but that was okay. Otto is way into comic books and looks it. Red has black hair and ironic parents. They've all been friends since kindergarten and they hang around our apartment so much, they don't seem like real boys to me. Or at least not the kind I find myself thinking about late at night.

And in the morning.

Afternoon, too.

"Hey," said Finn. He kept his hands in the pockets of his faded green cords so he wouldn't be tempted to pet Preston. Poor guy breaks out in hives every time he touches animal fur, which is a shame since he loves dogs so much.

Finn and I aren't identical twins, obviously. But we do have a lot in common—wavy brown hair, eyes that are green or hazel depending on the light, and a complexion that people call olive, like our dad's, who's Greek. We're both fairly tall for our age, although Finn is tall and skinny and I'm a little curvy. And we're both kind of quiet, but with Finn it comes across as intriguing. Girls always wonder what he's thinking about. My kind of quiet makes me invisible sometimes.

Except not when it really matters.

"Where's Dad?" I asked.

"He has a meeting in the city. Said he'd be back by six."

I checked my watch. It was only three thirty. "Cool, thanks."

"He wants us to make a salad for dinner, but will you do it?" Finn's question sounded more like an order.

"The whole thing?" I asked. "Isn't that blackmail?"

"No, I'm just saying—you've gotta be nice to your lookout." Finn headed back to his friends. Then he turned around to yell, "We can't just have grape tomatoes. That's cheating. You've gotta cut stuff up."

"I wasn't going to just do tomatoes!"

Finn didn't bother to reply. Not that he needed to. We both knew I couldn't be a dog walker without his help.

My mom isn't the problem. She's a lawyer in Manhattan and usually doesn't get home until after six. It's my dad I have to look out for. He makes documentaries, which are movies about things that are true, and they're usually too boring to see in a movie theater so people watch them at home on TV for free. It also means that sometimes—like now—he's unemployed. Or as he calls it, "in between jobs." So he hangs around the neighborhood a lot, and if he saw me walking some strange dog, well, it wouldn't be good.

My parents don't know I'm a dog walker. Sure, they know I walk Isabel's dog, but that was their idea and I do it as a favor. Meaning I don't get paid.

Mom and Dad don't know that I walk other dogs, like, in a professional capacity. And if they knew, they wouldn't like it because they're convinced that Finn and I are too young for jobs. They want us to focus on school and a few extracurricular activities of their choosing: kung fu on Saturdays, oil painting at the art museum on Sundays, and Italian-immersion class (including food, language, and art) in the summer.

It's not like I set out to lie to them exactly. I didn't even mean to start this business. The whole thing just kind of happened accidentally.

A few weeks ago, while I was out walking Preston, I ran into my old third grade teacher, Ms. Patel.

"Cute dog," she'd said as she bent down to scratch him behind his ears. "He must be a big eater."

"Don't know. I just walk him," I replied.

"So you're a dog walker?" she asked, and I told her yeah.

And before I could explain that I actually walk only Preston, Ms. Patel told me to call her Parminder and asked if I could fit her puggle into my schedule. She practically shoved her spare keys into my hands and I couldn't say no. Not because she was my favorite elementary school teacher, super generous with smiles and gold star stickers when that kind of thing actually mattered. And not just because she offered to pay me so well. I couldn't say no because her dog's name was Milo.

Aargh!

I tried not to think about the Pizza Den disaster as

Preston and I continued on through the park. We walked past the picnic grounds and along the edge of the baseball fields, stopping at the dog beach, which is actually just a slab of concrete leading into an artificial pond. A few lost-looking ducks floated on the murky surface.

Not being much of a water dog, Preston didn't seem to notice. He sniffed a nearby tree instead. Then he stalked a pigeon. I pulled him away and we kept walking. And walking.

"Let's go, Preston. I've still got two more dogs today."

Preston ignored me. Every time he paused to squat, he changed his mind. I was starting to lose patience when he found the perfect place. As he did his thing, I placed the plastic poop bag over my hand and got ready to scoop it up, hoping that Ivy—or worse, Milo—didn't walk by.

Luckily, the path was deserted except for two tired-looking moms, each pushing gigantic strollers up the hill. One of the strollers had twins in it. Girls, I assumed from their pink fleece jackets and purple booties. They were too young to protest over the matching outfits, but they'd do so eventually. This is a fact. And here's another one: Park Slope is crawling with twins. Sometimes literally.

When Preston finished, I bent down to scoop up his

mess and noticed something strange. It glittered in the afternoon sun. I don't normally study poop. Who would? But something about it struck me as odd. Odd as in blue and green and sparkly.

Sighing, I picked it up and put it in the bag. Mystery solved.

When we got back to Isabel's apartment I called, "How badly do you want that ring?"

But no one answered.

"Isabel?" I looked around but couldn't find her.

Weird, but I didn't give it much thought as I took off Preston's leash and placed it on the coatrack by the door.

Then I took out one of my note cards and a pen:

Doggie Deets

FROM THE DESK OF
MAGGIE BROOKLYN

Preston and I had fun in Prospect Park and I think we found your ring, too. Please see bag! (You also might want to put on some gloves and hold your nose.)

See you tomorrow,

Maggie

While my parents would be upset about my new business, they'd be happy that I finally found a use for the personalized stationery my aunt Sally gave me for my eighth birthday.

Yes, stationery for an eight-year-old. Obviously she doesn't have any children.

I capped my pen and headed for the door, glancing over my shoulder for one last look. Isabel wasn't anywhere to be seen, but her crutches? They were still lying on the couch, untouched.

Chapter 3

• • •

Unlike boy-Milo, dog-Milo is extremely easy to deal with. He's always happy to see me and he's very well behaved.

Bean is a different story. I picked her up as a client two weeks ago. Parminder referred me. She and Bean's owner, Cassie, live in the same building, except I can't walk her and Milo together because Bean tries to fight with every dog she sees. I guess no one told her she's a six-pound Maltese.

Another annoying thing about Bean—she wears a sweater. Not in the house; that would be too easy. Bean's owner has me dress her in a sweater before I take her outside. Although I've been told that this is strictly a cold weather–month policy. Once summer hits, I'll get to dress her in a T-shirt. Something to look forward to.

So after dropping off Milo, I walked up one flight of steps so I could fetch—and dress—Bean.

Her red-and-blue-striped cashmere hoodie sat folded on the kitchen table, still in its dry-cleaning bag. The dog has a nicer wardrobe than I do.

Since walking Bean is all about avoiding other animals, we headed away from the park. Everything went okay for a while. As soon as I spotted the flat-faced Boston terrier up ahead, I crossed the street. Bean didn't even notice him. Then I heard a kid on a scooter rolling up from behind. I picked up the pace and turned the corner because Bean also snarls at anything on wheels.

A minute later she sniffed at a half-eaten granola bar. "Let's go, Bean." I gave her leash a slight tug but Bean wouldn't budge. She's surprisingly strong for a six-pound animal. Stubborn, too.

After she finally did her thing, we turned around and headed back to her place. Before we even got close I spotted trouble up ahead: five humongous dogs pulling along one small woman. Like sled dogs racing, but without the sled.

Bean saw them, too, and she went crazy. Teeth bared and growling the most ferocious growl her half-pint-size body could muster, she strained to get at them.

And once the other dogs noticed her acting aggressive, they went crazy, too—barking, snarling, the works.

Their annoyed-looking walker had straight dark hair and short bangs. She wore hiking boots, faded jeans, and a gray sweatshirt with a big picture of a Dalmatian and the words DIAL-A-WALKER embroidered above it in red stitching.

"Can you move, please?" She barked even louder than her dogs. Also? Her "please" sounded more sarcastic than polite, like she owned the sidewalk and I should've known better than to trespass.

I scooped up Bean fast and turned to cross the street, but there was a truck coming. So the best thing I could do was step between two parked cars.

When she passed, the dark-haired woman squinted at me like she needed glasses, although she already wore a pair—rectangular ones with thin wire rims.

Bean growled and two of the woman's dogs snarled right back.

Suddenly one of them—a chubby chocolate Lab—broke free from his leash and darted straight at us.

I held Bean up high over my head, closed my eyes, and hoped for the best.

Luckily the dog ran right past. Turns out he was chasing a squirrel.

"Stop him!" the woman yelled, like a drill sergeant giving orders.

But it was all I could do to hang on to Bean, now flailing around like crazy.

The Labrador moved fast, darting across Garfield and up toward Prospect Park West—one of the busiest streets in the neighborhood.

I heard shouts.

Squealing brakes.

Skidding tires.

Then a horrific crash that seemed to reverberate for miles.

Next, silence. The scariest kind.

My heart ping-ponged in my chest.

The air reeked of burned rubber and it made me dizzy.

I squeezed my eyes shut tight and buried my face in Bean's neck, not minding the tickle of fur against my cheeks or the sharp perfume of her shampoo.

Doors slammed and people yelled.

I held my breath and did not move.

I was afraid to look—and once I finally did, I cried.

Chapter 4

◆ ◆ ◆

They were tears of relief, because the dog had made it.

The silver SUV was a different story. It was half on the sidewalk, a crushed garbage can under one tire, smoke billowing from its hood.

The owner was steaming worse than the car, because in swerving to avoid the dog, he'd run over the garbage can, then hit a lamppost.

"What's wrong with you, lady?" he screamed at the dark-haired woman.

"It's not my fault," she cried as she pulled a spare leash from her backpack and clipped it to the Lab's collar. (A jogger in green spandex had finally caught and returned the dog.) "The leash broke because he was pulling, and he was pulling because of her."

I thought it was kind of strange, blaming an innocent dog. That's before I noticed the woman's finger pointing at me, not Bean.

I took a step back. This so wasn't my fault, but before I could tell her, the guy said, "You've got to be kidding. You're gonna blame a kid?"

As he pulled out his cell phone and punched in some numbers, the dark-haired woman turned to me. "You need to be more careful with your dog. She could really get hurt. When you picked her up like that, my dogs thought she was a toy. That's why they got so crazy."

"They were acting crazy anyway," I said as I lowered Bean to the sidewalk. With her pink tongue thrust out, she marched back and forth like a hairy little soldier.

The chocolate Lab yawned and stretched out on the sidewalk. The other five dogs had calmed down, too. All sober like they knew how awful the accident could've been.

Meanwhile, I was still shaking. I took a deep, steady breath and willed my heart to slow down. "Anyway, she's not my dog. I just walk her."

The other walker did a double take and asked, "Wait. Is that Bean?"

I nodded. "You know her?"

"I didn't recognize her in the new sweater."

"It's cashmere."

"Of course it is," she snapped. "Where are you from?"

"Um, a few blocks away." I pointed in the general direction, not about to give up my address to a surly stranger.

The woman closed her eyes for a moment and huffed, impatient. "I mean who do you work for? Matilde's Mutts? Parker's Pooches? Tail Waggers Express?"

"What are you talking about?" I asked.

"Which dog-walking company are you with?"

"There are companies?"

"Of course there are companies."

She said it like I was stupid, but who ever heard of a dog-walking company? Not me. "I didn't know. I only walk a few dogs." This seemed to upset her even more.

"Great. You're not even a professional." She bent down to pet the Labrador. Then she spoke to him in a loud whisper. "I can't believe I got replaced by a child."

Okay, now she'd gone too far. "You know, I'm standing right here. I can hear you."

The woman groaned. "Don't take it so personally. It's just an expression. But how old are you, anyway?"

"I'm none of your business," I replied. "And a half."

She let out a short, angry breath, clearly not appreciating my sense of humor. "This is probably some fun little hobby for you, but I take my job seriously and I need these clients."

"I had no idea that you walked Bean. Cassie called

me out of the blue. I've never even met her in person. And Bean is just one dog."

"One dog today. Tomorrow it's gonna be five." She said it like she'd figured me out. Like I had some diabolical plan to systematically crush all the other dog-walking competition in town. But she couldn't have been further from the truth.

"No way can I walk five dogs. There'd be no time for my homework."

"Homework?" she spit out, furious now. "How did Cassie find you anyway? Craigslist? A flyer? Do you Tweet? All the dog walkers are on Twitter these days. It's so annoying."

"My old teacher Parminder recommended me. She lives in the same building as—"

"Parminder Patel?" she asked, interrupting.

I gulped and nodded.

"Milo's owner." She glared at me, incredulous. "So that means you stole him, too?"

Whoops. "I didn't steal him. She just asked me if I could walk him and—"

"Likely story," the woman huffed.

This seemed like the perfect time to disappear. "Um, gotta run," I said, backing away and pulling Bean along with me. Luckily, for once the little dog complied. We turned the corner and walked the three blocks to her building.

But before we made it inside, we ran into more trouble—this time in the form of a sticky blond toddler. He had strawberry ice cream in his hair, all over his face, and running down one arm. "Cookie!" he yelled as he ran over, blue-gray eyes as wide as nickels. Arms stretched out in front of him like a pint-size Frankenstein.

Bean bared her teeth. I tightened my grip on her leash and whispered, "Relax," but to no avail.

"Cookie!" he screamed again, even though by now he was right next to us.

I patted my empty pockets. "I don't have any on me."

The kid glanced at me, seemingly unimpressed.

It was one thing for the angry dog walker to make me feel dumb, but a three-year-old? "What?" I asked.

He pointed at Bean. "Dat's Cookie!"

"Oh! You mean she looks like your dog, Cookie?" I asked. "That's funny. Her name is Bean, actually."

"Beckett!" yelled the kid's mom as she hurried over. She had curly blond hair just like her son's, only longer and cleaner. "You can't run away like that!"

The kid took a step closer.

Bean growled and I understood why. From her point of view, Beckett was a clumsy giant. And only two steps away from crushing her.

"Beckett, please." His mom dropped to her knees,

placed her hands on his shoulders, and looked into his eyes. "That's not Cookie, honey."

"Yes, Cookie." He screwed up his mouth and stomped his foot. The heel of his silver high-top flashed red. Light-up shoes—Finn and I used to have them. I didn't realize they were still in style.

His mom cringed and looked up at me. "He thinks that's our old dog," she explained, and then turned back to her son. "Cookie went bye-bye to the farm. Remember?"

"Bye-bye, Cookie." The kid opened and closed his hand in front of Bean's face—some approximation of a wave. "Why you leave me? Because of the gum?"

"We've been over this, honey. Cookie forgives you for putting all that gum in her fur, but she still had to go to the farm," his mom said.

The kid looked from his mom to Bean. "Farm?" he asked.

She winked at me. "Yes, Cookie went to the farm."

According to my parents, Finn and I've had six goldfish that have also gone to the farm. Wonder if it's the same one . . .

At least Beckett seemed convinced—for the moment. His mom stood, took his hand, and led him away.

But before I could walk much farther, Beckett broke free, raced back, and got right in Bean's face. "Come back," he said. "I won't pull your tail no more. Or eat your food."

Bean snapped, barely missing Beckett's cheek and coming close enough to make him scream.

Beckett's mom scooped him up in her arms—much to Beckett's chagrin. "No more throw you in toilet!" Beckett shouted over her shoulder.

"Sorry to bother you," his mom said as she struggled to contain her flailing kid. "She really does look a lot like Cookie, though. It's been weeks since she, well, went to the farm, but Beckett still talks about her."

"That's so sad. Was there an, um, accident?" I asked, shuddering at the thought.

Beckett's mom sighed. "No, she had a rare heart defect. We tried surgery but it was too late."

"Surgery," Beckett repeated.

"Yes, honey. Remember? Poor Cookie had surgery, and instead of coming home she decided to go to the farm."

"Horsies there, too?" asked Beckett.

"Yes, probably," said his mom.

"And sheep?"

"Yup." She nodded.

"Let's visit," said Beckett.

"Oh dear." His mom cringed and furrowed her brow. "No, we can't. It's too far. But I'll take you to the zoo later, okay? Now say bye-bye."

"Bye-bye, Cookie!" said Beckett. And he kept saying it, even after he and his mom turned the corner.

Sad, but at the same time, almost funny, too. At least that's what I'd thought at the time. Turns out I never should've laughed.

Beckett knew exactly what he was talking about.

Chapter 5

• • •

"Nice salad," Finn mumbled at dinner that night as he stabbed a grape tomato with his fork.

"Thank you." I smiled sweetly, ignoring the sarcasm.

He scoffed, but I knew he'd never give me up. Not to our parents.

"How was the math quiz?" Dad asked.

"Math-y," I replied.

"Numbers all over the place," Finn agreed.

"Yeah, that's exactly what I wanted to know," Dad replied.

"How'd your meeting go?" Mom asked him.

"You know. Lots of talk." Dad shrugged. Then when no one reacted he said, "Actually, I got the job."

"That's great," I said. And I meant it. With Dad working again, I wouldn't have to worry about avoiding him during my dog-walking hours.

"It is." Dad's whole face brightened. "The project is interesting, too. I'll be producing a documentary about the Brooklyn Dodgers."

"That sounds fun. Congratulations!" Mom raised her glass of lemon-lime seltzer and we all clinked glasses.

Then she turned to me and Finn. "I still need to call the Cake Man for Saturday. Are we going with the usual?"

"Yup," I said. Finn nodded.

We were turning twelve that weekend and we always have a joint birthday party with a cake that's half vanilla for Finn and half chocolate for me. Raspberry filling because neither of us cares much about it, equally.

"And it's eight people?" she asked.

"Um, ten, actually," said Finn.

"Who else did you invite?" I asked.

Finn didn't reply. In fact, he didn't even look at me. That's how I knew I wasn't going to like his answer. Not when we were supposed to have three friends each, and Finn had nearly doubled his list without even asking me. Not only would my friends be totally outnumbered, I seriously doubted Finn had invited anyone cool. He'd probably asked a couple guys from GameStop—the video-game store where Finn always spends his allowance. Unless he'd invited some of the geeks from Galaxy Comics. I couldn't decide which would be worse.

"Finn?"

He stared at his empty salad plate, too silent.

"Not Brady," I said. Brady is into comic books and video games but his real claim to fame is being able to swear in twelve languages. It's funny the first time you hear it. But he's been demonstrating his skills at least twice a day since school started three weeks ago. And it gets old—fast.

"It's not Brady," said Finn.

"Phew." I breathed a sigh of relief.

"It's Eve, Katie, and Ivy." He mumbled it so I barely heard.

"Ha. Very funny."

Finn didn't laugh. No one did.

I glared at him from across the table. "You are kidding."

He shook his head ever so slightly.

"Finn!"

"It's no big deal."

"It's a huge deal!" I looked to my parents. "This can't happen. You can't let him do this."

"It's not just your party," Finn reminded me. Which was so unnecessary, because obviously if it were just my party there wouldn't be any vanilla in the cake.

Not that I could even bring myself to care about that at the moment. "But you're not even friends with them!"

"No yelling at the table," Dad said.

"I'm not yelling!" I yelled. Then hearing myself, I swallowed hard and tried—unsuccessfully—to relax. Problem was, my whole throat felt tight and tears pricked the corners of my eyes. And now I was embarrassed, because I didn't want to totally lose it in front of my family. Not over Ivy.

I looked from my mom to my dad. "You can't let him ruin my birthday."

"This is between you two," said Dad.

I turned to Finn, half wishing I could crawl across the table, grab him by the shoulders, and shake some sense into him. But I knew better. I could hand Finn a clue on a silver platter and he wouldn't know what to do with it. "How did this happen?" I asked.

Finn shrugged. "Dante was supposed to come but his parents are making him go look at leaves in Vermont instead. So that meant I could have one more person and Otto likes Eve and he asked me to invite her so I did. And she said, 'Can I bring Ivy and Katie?' and I said, 'Sure.'"

He spoke so quickly I knew he felt guilty. "You said, 'Sure,'" I repeated.

"She put me on the spot," said Finn. Then he turned

to our parents. "I know we were supposed to keep the guest list small and I tried—I really did—but it was impossible to say no. So if you want to ground me or something, go ahead."

Finn hung his head in pretend shame, and I couldn't believe my parents bought his story. But they did.

"Of course we're not going to ground you," said Dad, clapping Finn on the back all buddy-buddy. "It sounds like Eve didn't give you any real choice, so don't worry about it. The more the merrier."

Finn's display was so pathetic I couldn't help but yell, "Unbelievable!"

Sighing, Mom turned to me. "I know it's not easy, Maggie, but try to be the bigger person."

Whatever that meant.

"Let's have separate parties," I said. "Finn can have Saturday and I'll ask my friends to come on Sunday instead."

"But the party's only two days away," said Mom.

"My friends won't care."

"Maggie," said Dad, "two parties isn't going to happen. Maybe next year, but for now, no." The finality in his tone told me to drop it. And that's when I figured out the real issue: money. As in, a lack of it. My parents couldn't afford two parties. Normally, no biggie. Finn's friends are cool (for the most part) and I'm used to sharing. But with Ivy? There's no way.

"I'll pay for it," I said without thinking.

"It's not about the money," said Mom.

"And it's not like you could pay anyway," said Finn, giving me a meaningful look from across the table.

He had a point. My small allowance was enough for an after-school slice of pizza or ice-cream cone (without sprinkles). A movie on a Saturday night if I saved up. It's not like I could tell our parents about my dog-walking money.

But still, I had to do something. I couldn't just sit around and smile and make small talk as if Saturday wasn't going to be the worst day of my life. "Okay, fine, but can I go to Lucy's?" I asked.

"It's a school night," said Mom.

"I'll be home in an hour." I stood up and cleared my plate, thinking that if I pretended they'd already said yes, they'd think they had. And it worked.

"You hardly ate anything," said Dad as I made my way out.

"Yeah, Finn kinda made me lose my appetite."

Not exactly the truth, but enough to get me out of there.

Chapter 6

◆ ◆ ◆

I could smell the sautéed onions even before Lucy opened her front door. And once she did, the scent made my mouth water.

"Hungry?" she asked.

My new favorite question. "Starving," I replied and followed her to the kitchen.

The best thing about being friends with Lucy— besides the fact that she's super sweet and hilarious and would never ditch me for someone (supposedly) cooler—is the fact that her parents own a small chain of restaurants: two in Brooklyn and one over the bridge in Alphabet City. They're always experimenting with new recipes and looking for taste testers. Their food is Vietnamese-Peruvian fusion, just like Lucy.

And after my disastrous day with the dogs and Finn's news about the dreaded Ivy, which only ruined my appetite briefly, I really needed a snack.

"Maggie, you're just in time," said Lucy's dad, Chuck, as he spooned something from his frying pan onto a pale green lettuce leaf. "This is pork belly with scallions— my great grandmother's recipe. It's a little spicy, but you don't mind spicy, do you?"

"Nope. Not at all."

Lucy scrunched up her nose as I reached for the plate. She refuses to eat anything that's not grilled cheese or spaghetti with red sauce. Something her parents would be more upset about, probably, except that until recently she'd only taken her pasta with butter.

"Mmm." I chewed and swallowed. "So good."

"But is it better than the ginger duck wrapped in cilantro-infused rice paper?" asked her mom, Vanessa.

"Hello?" Lucy interrupted. "Are you done using my friend as a guinea pig?"

"Unless you want me to sample some dessert." I looked around the kitchen. "Because I'm all for that."

"Try us next week," said Vanessa. "We need to iron out the entrées first."

"You girls are dismissed," Chuck joked, like it was time for recess.

"Finally." Lucy grabbed my hand and pulled me toward the staircase.

Lucy lives six houses down from me in an identical brownstone, but her family has four whole floors, not just one. We have the same bedroom, too, except Lucy's seems gigantic because she has it all to herself. I share mine with Finn, which is not as weird as it sounds. A huge bookshelf splits our room right down the middle and offers plenty of privacy. There's a big bay window that looks out onto Garfield Place, and we each have half a view.

"So, you and Milo. Tell me everything," Lucy said once we were in her room and out of earshot.

I stifled a groan. With everything else going on, I'd completely forgotten about the Milo mess.

"Let's just say that I've secured my place in the Pizza Den Hall of Shame."

Lucy's eyes got wide. "You didn't pull an Amber Greyson, did you?"

"It wasn't *that* bad," I said. (Amber puked up something purple there last spring.)

"And you stayed away from the chili peppers?"

"Come on, Lucy. Give me a little credit." I flopped down into her blue beanbag chair.

She sat in the green one across from me. "Well, you're being so mysterious. What am I supposed to think?"

"I don't know—maybe that I'd never try to impress Milo by sticking hot peppers up my nose. Especially since Paul Livingston ended up in the emergency room for that just two weeks ago."

Lucy shuddered. "I heard he still gets teary-eyed whenever he sneezes."

I blinked. "I get teary-eyed just thinking about it."

"So what happened?" asked Lucy. "I've been sending you good vibes all afternoon. I couldn't even focus on my violin lesson. Mrs. Tamagachi was all, 'Lucy, if you don't pay attention, you'll never make it to first chair.' As if I care!"

I stood up and walked over to Lucy's owl collection—so big it takes up an entire wall-size bookcase. She's got owl everything: mugs, pencils, stuffed animals, pillows, ceramic figurines—both life-size and miniature and one with real feathers. I picked up an owl egg timer. "Is this new?" I asked. "It's cute."

Lucy stared at me. "Why are you stalling?"

"I'm not."

"Maggie!"

I put away the egg timer and sat down on her futon couch. "Nothing to tell. Everything's a mess and I'm super embarrassed and the Pizza Den was just the beginning."

I told Lucy the whole story: Milo and his iPod, the Ivy intrusion, the car wreck, getting chewed out by some stranger who thought I was bad for her business. And how my birthday party had been sabotaged. "Ivy's like this giant stink bomb that's gonna poison the whole scene."

"She is awful," said Lucy. "What was Finn thinking?"

"He wasn't," I said.

"You don't think he likes her, do you?"

"My brother can be pretty clueless sometimes, but he's not stupid. Otto likes Eve, apparently. He asked Finn to invite her, and you know how the three of them can't do anything unless they're all together. Like they share a brain."

"Oh."

"I'm serious. Eve and Katie can't even buy a pack of gum without clearing it with Ivy first. I mean, if you're—"

"I get it," Lucy interrupted. She twisted her wavy black hair into a messy bun. "So what are you going to do about Milo?"

"Nothing."

"But you've been crushing on him since forever."

"Not forever," I said.

"Fine. Since you saw him leaning against his locker that first day he transferred, but that was months ago. When we were sixth graders. And what did you say the other day? About how you were sick of watching stuff happen to other people? How you wanted something to happen to you?"

"Public humiliation isn't exactly what I had in mind."

"Well, what about our promise?"

This past summer, we'd vowed to do everything possible to get boyfriends this year. (Way embarrassing but true.) So far, Lucy couldn't figure out who to like, but she promised that once she did, she'd make her move. And as for me? Well, obviously I needed a new tactic.

"What time is it?" I glanced up at her wall clock, a pink owl with eyes that moved from side to side with each passing second. Lucy calls her Ms. Owlet Supreme. I'm not sure why, but her wings told me I was ten minutes late. "I've gotta go."

"Or do you just not want to answer me?" asked Lucy.

"I can't deny that." I stood up. "But I do need to get home. You know what they say—time flies when you're avoiding your brother."

Lucy tilted her head to one side and flashed me a skeptical glance. "Who says that?"

"I do."

As I headed for the door, Lucy called, "Wait, before you leave, tell me what you think of this." She pulled something green and white and lumpy out of her knitting bag. "Do you think Finn will like it?"

"Depends. What is it?"

Lucy folded it carefully in her lap. "Half a scarf. The rest will be done by the weekend, probably. Depending on whether or not I go back and fix the crooked stitches in the middle. He probably wouldn't even notice, right? Or if he did, maybe he'd think it's part of the design?"

"Finn's not so into shopping for clothes," I said. "Accessories, especially. And I don't think he even knows about Etsy. I know you've been trying to expand your customer base, but I don't think this is the way to—"

Lucy cut me off. "I'm not trying to sell it. I just thought I'd give it to him."

"Oh. Why?"

"For his birthday," said Lucy.

"No one's supposed to bring us gifts, remember? My parents' idea, obviously. It's like my whole family is conspiring to make my birthday stink."

"It won't be that bad. And I wasn't going to bring it to the party. I'll give it to him some other time. Since I made one for you. It seemed like . . . I don't know." Lucy didn't finish her thought. I couldn't believe she was pulling this.

There's nothing more annoying than people who think Finn and I should wear matching, or even coordinating, outfits. And Lucy should know better. "We are not going to wear *twin* scarves."

"This is completely different." Lucy seemed insulted. "Yours is turquoise and purple striped."

"Yeah—the key word is 'striped.' "

"You're too sensitive, Maggie. Striped patterns are

my favorite. That's all I do, practically." She bit her bottom lip. "Anyway, it was only a thought."

"Keep thinking," I said as I headed for the door. "See you tomorrow."

Chapter 7

. . .

When I went to collect Preston after school on Friday, I found Isabel's apartment in shambles. The couch cushions were askew, clothes were spilled from her coat closet, and her living room rug was half rolled up, revealing a patch of wood floor that was distinctly lighter than the rest.

"What happened?" I asked Preston, who was lounging on his dog bed under the window.

His bored expression told me—quite clearly—nothing new.

I once read somewhere that dogs have a sixth sense about danger. When they get scared, their fur spikes and their tails curl between their legs. Sometimes they bark like crazy. And if things seem really bad, they'll whimper.

Preston looked perfectly at home, which should've brought relief.

But the place was so eerily silent, it made my spine tingle. It just didn't make any sense. Where did Isabel go when she disappeared? How could someone so loud and large seemingly vanish in an apartment so small and cramped?

"Hello?" I called out in vain. "Isabel?"

My voice seemed to echo. But it had to be my imagination. That's what I told myself, anyway.

Preston stood, stretched, and lumbered over.

"Where is she?" I asked him as I crouched down to scratch his neck with both hands.

Suddenly someone knocked on the door. It made me jump. And the next thing I knew, something creaked and slammed and then Isabel came waltzing out of her bedroom, like everything was completely normal.

"Oh, hi, Maggie." She seemed surprised to see me, yet managed to shift from a healthy stride to a painful-looking limp in half a heartbeat. "You're early today. I didn't even hear you come in."

I shrugged, not wanting to tell her my true reason for being ahead of schedule. I was avoiding the Pizza Den. No way could I face Milo after yesterday.

Isabel hobbled past me to open the door.

It was Chloe, who lives on the second floor. Chloe's a full-time librarian and a part-time drummer in a retro punk band called the Dewey Decibels. They perform every weekend—sometimes in the city and sometimes in Brooklyn. She keeps inviting me to shows but they always happen past my bedtime. Plus, I'm only twelve (or will be tomorrow) and I can't get into bars.

I have heard her sing, though. Usually when she's in the shower because the sound travels up along the pipes. Her voice is so pretty and professional-sounding, sometimes I think it's the radio I'm listening to.

"Hi, Chloe," said Isabel. "Lovely of you to stop by. Can I get you some coffee?"

"No, I'm off caffeine, plus I'm already late for rehearsal." Chloe waved her drumsticks as if she needed proof. Her hair was long, blue-black, and shiny, and it bounced whenever she moved. "I need to talk to you about something—mice."

Isabel gasped and brought one hand to her chest, like the mere mention of any rodent would send a thousand swarming. "Dreadful creatures." She shuddered.

Chloe nodded. "I agree. And I'm pretty sure they've moved in."

"You mean here?" Isabel asked. "Impossible."

"I heard *something* scurrying around in the walls last night."

"Are you sure it wasn't the television?"

Chloe nodded. "Positive. There was definitely movement. It sounded pretty loud. Kind of clumsy, too."

Isabel reeled back as if offended. "Well, I can't say I have any idea what you're talking about."

When Isabel gets upset, she cops a British accent, and this was one of those times.

Chloe must have known this, too, because she didn't even blink. "They might even be raccoons. My boss lives on Fifteenth Street and she found five of them in her basement one night. It was quite the ordeal."

"Sounds like it," said Isabel. "It's lucky there aren't any here."

"As far as you know," said Chloe. "But you might want to investigate. Especially in that back bedroom—the one with the bay window and the crawl space—"

"There's no crawl space there—just a door that's been sealed shut for years," Isabel said, interrupting.

"I know," said Chloe. "But I'm telling you, that's where I heard the noise. Maybe some mice got in."

"Impossible! That wall is solid. And if this is an attempt to withhold your rent, I'll have you know that you're paying well below the market rate because you're a fellow artist. This building has a long tradition of housing creative types. Did I ever tell you about Al Flosso, the Coney Island Fakir?"

"You mean Brooklyn's most amazing and under-rated magician?" Chloe asked.

"You've heard of him?" Isabel asked, excited.

"Yes," said Chloe. "From you."

"He built this grand residence," Isabel went on, sweeping one crutch through the air with dramatic flair.

"Was trained by Houdini within these walls. If only he hadn't made such an unfortunate choice of a stage name. Houdini—now that's a memorable name. But Al Flosso, the Fakir? At best, it's laughable. And at worst, forgettable."

"I know, I know," Chloe said tiredly, like she'd heard it all before. (And I knew precisely how she felt.) "But this problem is only going to get worse if you don't address it now."

"Maybe it was Glen," Isabel said. "He can be loud and clumsy."

Glen lives on the third floor. He's tall and skinny with a shaved head, and Isabel's right. He's always dropping things. And lugging his clunky bike up and down the stairs. Glen is a bike messenger/guitar player who gives music lessons out of his apartment—another noisy venture.

"It wasn't Glen," said Chloe. "Not unless his students happen to be rodents."

Isabel frowned. "Well, that wouldn't make any sense. I hardly think any rodent could afford his rate. Not to mention hold a guitar. They don't have opposable thumbs, you know."

"That's not what I . . ." Chloe stopped herself and took a deep breath. "Look, would you please call an exterminator? Or at least set some traps?"

"I'll look into it," said Isabel. "But really, dear, I don't think you have anything to worry about. I'm sure this is all in your pretty little head and whatever you heard won't be back."

Chloe blinked curiously. "Okay, but I don't know how you can sound so sure . . ."

Isabel stood as tall as she could while also leaning on crutches. "I'm quite confident that in the twenty-five years I've lived here, these walls have seen a lot of things, but mice are not among them. Now, did I ever tell you about the time I starred in a show opposite Nathan Lane? He once—"

"Yeah, you did," said Chloe as she headed for the door. "And it's a fascinating story. More fascinating every time I hear it. I wish I had time now, but I really need to run. See ya, Maggie."

" 'Bye!" I waved.

Once Chloe was gone, Isabel turned to me and said, "Mice! Can you imagine?"

I shivered involuntarily. I didn't want to be the type of girl who got queasy in the face of mice, but I couldn't help it. The icky creatures creeped me out! So I changed the subject. "What did you lose this time?" I asked, pointing to the mess.

Isabel said, "Nothing. I'm just doing a little spring cleaning."

"It's almost October."

"Never too early to get started. Or too late, depending on how you look at things. Now where was I? Oh, yes. Nathan Lane."

"So you found the ring yesterday. Right?" I asked to distract her, but I also wanted to make sure.

Isabel scrunched up her nose. "I did. Thank you for bringing it back, Maggie. I'm so grateful. You really have a gift, you know? Luckily, the ring is undamaged and I now know that Preston has superb taste in jewelry."

"And it looks like your knee is getting better."

Isabel held out one leg and stared in contemplation. "Oh, it comes and goes. The doctor tells me to take things slow, which reminds me—I made an appointment to get Preston's nails clipped on Monday, but I don't think I can manage. Would you mind taking him?"

I played along even though I knew Isabel could walk just fine. "At what time does he need to go?"

"Three o'clock. The place is right down the street on Sixth Avenue and First Street."

"Is that some new vet?" I asked, since last time I took Preston to a place on Prospect Park West.

"It is. His old place was so expensive. I'm sure they were overcharging me, and I just got this coupon in the mail." Isabel handed me a postcard—orange with bold black letters that read, NOW OPEN FOR BUSINESS: DR. REESE, VETERINARIAN. KIND. GENTLE. REASONABLE RATES.

"Sure, I'll take him." I pocketed the card.

"Thank you, dear. I don't know what I'd do without you."

Probably fake-limp less, I thought but didn't say. Instead I found Preston's leash underneath a pile of sequined throw pillows, clipped it to his collar, and headed out the door.

Chapter 8

· · ·

**FROM THE DESK OF
MAGGIE BROOKLYN**

Bean seems to be having a hard time walking in her new cape. She keeps tripping on all the extra material. I think it put her in a rotten mood. More rotten than usual, I mean. You might want to think about returning it. Or at least getting the thing tailored. Other than that, she did her business, gobbled down her snack, and only snarled at two people and three other dogs. So all in all, we had fun. Thanks for the cash.

See ya Monday!
Maggie

For all the trouble I have with Bean, I do appreciate that her owner, Cassie, pays me with crisp new bills every Friday. It almost seems like they should be worth more than wrinkled old ones. On the other hand, Cassie and

Parminder pay me the same amount of money per walk, and Bean is way harder to deal with than Milo, so I guess it all balances out.

I finished my note to Cassie and hurried downstairs to pick up Milo—my last walk of the week.

"Hey, guy!" I said as I opened the door.

As usual, he greeted me with a cheerful bark and a vigorous tail wag. Then he jumped. "Easy, buddy," I said, and I crouched down to his level so I could pet him some more. But then he wouldn't stop licking my face, so I stood up.

Once I got him to sit still long enough for me to clip his leash to his collar, we walked into the park at Third Street. It's my favorite entrance because of the gigantic bronze panthers flanking each side. They look so dignified up on their tall white columns, chests puffed, gazes forward, super alert like they're protecting the whole park somehow, at least in spirit.

We walked straight through them and headed past the playground on the right. A thick row of trees separated us, so even though we couldn't see the children, we could hear their shouts and laughter drifting through the leaves.

Farther in, the smells of burgers and hot dogs wafted over from the barbecue pits by the Picnic House, making my stomach grumble and probably Milo's, too, since he kept trying to tug me closer.

"No, we're not gonna go there," I said, pulling on his leash. "And in case you were worried, don't be. Hot dogs aren't really made out of dogs."

Sometimes even I'm surprised by how corny my jokes are. Good thing no one heard. No one with opposable thumbs, that is. And there I go again. But I guess it's okay to think dumb thoughts sometimes. It's the saying them out loud part that gets me in trouble. *I walk a dog named Milo*, for example? Why had that seemed like the right thing to say?

I hurried Milo past the Picnic House. He soon grew distracted by a large black mutt. The two dogs sniffed each other a bit. Then we moved on, Milo stopping to investigate the occasional tree, and me kicking the occasional rock.

Once Milo did what he needed to do, I still didn't feel like going home, so we headed over to the nature trail. It's on the opposite side of the park and is dense with trees. The farther in you go, the more shaded it becomes. By the time we got to the thick of it, the air felt damp and the temperature dropped by what seemed like ten degrees. I felt as if I'd strolled into a fairy-tale forest. As long as I overlooked the smashed beer cans and random empty packages of Fritos, that is.

The waterfall flowed nearby, but otherwise all was silent save for my footsteps and the quick pitter-patter of Milo's paws against the dirt. It was peaceful. Comforting, even.

At least until I heard something strange up ahead—first just a rustling. Then some twigs snapped.

Suddenly Milo stopped sniffing and raised his head. Ears perked, he pulled me forward with a force so strong I had no choice but to follow.

As we turned the corner I saw what the fuss was about. Milo had found another dog—a little fluffy white one. Not a poodle, exactly, but still French and fancy looking. I exhaled in relief, not realizing I'd been holding my breath.

"Hey there," I said to the dog, trying to figure out what breed it was. Maltese? Bichon frise? Shih tzu? Or some crazy new hybrid? I couldn't tell and was so focused that I didn't even notice the guy at the other end of the leash.

Not until I heard the sharp gasp of breath. Clearly someone was surprised to see me, and not pleasantly so.

I looked up suddenly, and I locked eyes with him— Milo!

Yeah, *that* Milo.

My first instinct was to run. Hide. Just disappear. But it was too late.

Obviously, he saw me. And for some reason, he seemed more freaked out than I was. His eyes darted from side to side, like he was searching for an escape route. But we were on a narrow path and there was nowhere to go.

He had no choice but to move forward. Something he did with dread, like I was Vice Principal Mackey and he'd just gotten caught flushing firecrackers down the teachers' lounge toilet.

Which, let me assure you, did wonders for my self-esteem.

I mean, obviously Milo thought I was a total freaka-zoid or he wouldn't look so panicked, right? Why, oh why had I bothered to try and speak to him at Pizza Den yesterday? What made me think I ever had a chance?

And while I was asking myself questions, how come all the pretend conversations I had with Milo in my head were so much easier—so much better—than our real-life actual ones?

I guess I just preferred admiring Milo from afar. Something I wished I could do at the moment. But he was already looking at me, so I couldn't turn around.

We had to speak. Yet, so far all I could manage was a gulp.

I told myself to act normal. Which is a surefire way to look weird.

As in way dorky.

I smiled. Then I worried my smile was too big. Or maybe too nervous looking. So I stopped smiling. But I didn't want to appear unfriendly. So I took a step forward and he did, too. And then we were so close one of us had to say something, and it didn't seem like it was going to be him.

"You never told me you had a dog," I blurted out. "Hello" would've been more appropriate, I guess, but no one ever accused me of being the smoothest conversationalist.

I swallowed hard.

"Hey, Maggie," he said carefully.

"You know my name?" I asked—again with the absolute worst response.

Milo smiled—small with his mouth closed. "Sure, from science." He pushed his bangs out of his eyes.

"Oh yeah. I know. I was just kidding." I forced a laugh, hoping he wouldn't notice that I hadn't exactly been funny.

"So this is Milo?" he asked.

"How did you know?"

"You told me you walked a puggle back at the Pizza Den, remember?"

"Oh yeah." So he *had* heard me.

"Or is this another puggle? Do you specialize in the breed?"

Was he joking? Probably. But I couldn't tell and I didn't want to take the risk, so I answered him honestly. "No, I walk all sorts. A Maltese, an Irish wolfhound . . .

and um, well, actually those are my only three clients right now."

Milo's mouth twisted up in a way that told me he *had* been kidding. So now he probably thought I had no sense of humor.

"He's cute," he said, smiling down at Milo.

"Thanks," I said. "I mean, he's not mine or anything. I just walk him. But he's my favorite. One of my favorites, anyway. I actually like all the dogs I walk." Just then the image of a snarling Bean dressed in a sparkly sequined sweater-vest popped into my head. "Well, most anyway. Who's yours?"

Milo didn't answer me. Not right away. Instead he looked around, like he was afraid someone would see us together.

"Know what?" he asked, taking a step back and tugging lightly on the leash. "I forgot but I'm really late for this, um, thing. So I'll see you later."

He turned around and took off without another word. Running so fast, his little dog could barely keep up.

Chapter 9

• • •

An hour later I found Finn in our room, kicking back on his bed and working on his homework.

Moby's new album streamed from his laptop.

"Did you buy this?" I asked.

"Red burned me a copy," he replied.

"Nice."

Red's way into indie bands and he keeps us up-to-date on new music, which is cool, for the most part. But he can be a music snob sometimes, and I'm still a little annoyed with him for making fun of my Taylor Swift CD last month. He didn't say much—just held it up with two fingers, like it was a piece of moldy cheese, and asked, "What's this?" in a super-snooty tone.

And Finn let out a laugh and said, "Maggie's." Like he couldn't believe it, either, which wasn't fair because I've caught him humming along to her music on more than one occasion. I could've said so but didn't because I'm nice like that.

I knelt down in front of our fireplace, where Finn and I keep our most valuable stuff. The fireplace doesn't work—it's only decorative (something we discovered a few years ago when we tried making s'mores in it). But that just makes it an excellent hiding place. Pretty, too. It's cast iron and gray and the door has a tin plate with a cool pattern stamped into it—little suns inside square boxes.

The facade is painted shut, or at least it looks that way. But if you know how to turn the handle—with a slight wiggle and some force, but not too much, while pressing down on the upper left-hand corner—the door swings open in a snap, revealing a small space that's perfect for storing Finn's first edition comic books and my cigar box, which has not actually contained cigars in ages.

The box was a gift from Ivy—from years ago, obviously. And it's where I keep everything I need for my dog-walking business:

Three sets of keys, color-coded and linked to a
     carabiner (I don't put names or addresses
     on the keys because if they ever got lost or
     stolen, I'd have a big problem.)

Spare leash

Plastic bags

Doggie Deets stationery

Pen

Spare pen

Treats

Portable bowl

And most important, my dog-walking cash

I unloaded my backpack, added this week's earnings to the already sizable pile, and secured the money with a red rubber band.

"I made flash cards for the new Spanish vocab. Want to quiz each other?"

Finn offering to study with me on a Friday night? Bizarro! Also weird—Finn usually waits for me to make flash cards. But this was no random act of kindness. Obviously, my brother had a major case of guilt about ruining my birthday. And I wasn't about to let him do me any favors just so he could feel better about himself.

"No thanks," I said coldly. "I'd rather make my own."

"So you're still mad," said Finn. "It's not my fault. Eve put me on the spot and you'd have done the same thing."

I glared at him.

"Well, maybe not with Eve. I get that. But if it were anyone else . . ."

I shook my head. "You can't even compare because you have no Ivy equivalent."

"So now you're annoyed with me for not having enemies?"

It's true—everyone likes Finn. But the way he said this made me sound so petty. "That's not what I meant."

Finn tapped his pencil against his Spanish book. My Spanish book, actually.

"I still don't get why you have to hate her so much."

I stopped myself from saying, "She started it," because it sounded too babyish, although it's completely accurate. "It's complicated," I said instead.

It was enough to get Finn off my back. And it was the truth.

Of course, at the time, I didn't know how true it was.

Or how much more complicated things were about to get.

Chapter 10

◆ ◆ ◆

Turning twelve means you're too old to have a party organized by your parents—with activities and games and goodie bags—and too young to know what you're supposed to be doing at a party when no one is organizing it for you.

It's like one minute you're knocking down a piñata and playing Duck Duck Goose and Musical Chairs, and the next minute you're supposed to be playing Spin the Bottle and Seven Minutes in the Closet and Five Minutes in Heaven. Or maybe it's Five Minutes in the Closet and Seven Minutes in Heaven? Actually, they're probably the same game and "closet" and "heaven" can be used interchangeably, but only in this one case.

I cannot be certain, though, because I've never actually seen any of these games go down in real life. Finn and I had only heard rumors and we were not going to be the first of our friends to suggest playing. Because what if we went about it wrong? I couldn't really imagine what wrong would look like, but it seemed like the kind of thing that would be hard to live down, so we were playing things safe. This was strictly a coed pizza party, with no kissing, or at least no kissing games.

Of course, that didn't mean we needed our parents hanging around. As soon as our dad headed out to pick up the food, Finn and I looked to our mom. "Okay, okay. I'm going," she said, holding up her hands. "Now as agreed, your father and I will stay in our room."

"Behind closed doors," Finn added.

"Yes, behind closed doors. You won't even know we're home unless we hear something strange."

"Define strange," said Finn.

"Something that sounds like trouble," she said.

"That's still pretty vague," I had to point out.

"Don't you think your father and I have better things to do than eavesdrop on our children?"

Neither Finn nor I answered.

"Gee, thanks," Mom said as she shook her head. "I'm outta here." She squeezed my shoulder on her way out, adding, "Don't forget to have fun," with a meaningful wink.

That morning, over breakfast, my mom had insisted that Ivy would only bother me if I let her. Also, that nothing would bother Ivy more than being ignored because, in being so mean, she's merely acting out for attention and blah, blah, blah . . . Obviously it was advice she got from a book on "girl empowerment." The kind that's useless in real life—not that I'd tell her. Better to act like I was totally swayed, otherwise she might try and get *me* to read one of those books.

So when Mom winked, I gave her a half smile, which might also be interpreted as a smirk, not bothering to point out that if someone needs to be reminded to have fun, the chances of that person actually having fun are probably not great.

As soon as the doorbell rang at five after, my stomach cramped with panic. I guess I felt nervous that Ivy might show up first and make everything awkward. At the same time, I felt totally annoyed with myself for caring.

Except I didn't need to stress because it was only Red, and I should've guessed. Red's always on time or early, which is funny because he lives the farthest away—all the way in Windsor Terrace, on the other side of the park.

"Yo," he said when I answered the door.

Finn and his friends all started saying "Yo" to one another last spring and apparently it hasn't gotten old— at least as far as they're concerned.

"Hey, Red," I replied.

His black hair looked moplike-shaggy, as usual, and he was dressed in his uniform of dark skinny jeans with a silver wallet chain and a T-shirt from some obscure indie band show. Little round glasses, too. Red often wears sunglasses indoors and I used to think it was cool, but ever since the Taylor Swift incident I'm wondering if it's actually kind of pretentious.

"Happy birthday squared." He flashed me a peace sign and a goofy, all-braces grin. He knows we're not into any cutesy twins stuff, but he likes to tease us anyway.

Finn was standing right behind me, and he scoffed. "How long did it take you to come up with that one?" he asked.

"I only just now thought of it," Red said.

He and Finn slapped each other five. Then the slap turned into a handshake, snap, fist-bump, and something else that got too complicated for me to follow.

The doorbell rang again, and this time it was Otto, who said "Yo" and went through the same slap, shake, snap, fist-bump thing with Finn and then with Red and when he turned to me I just waved.

Beatrix came next, and for that I was glad.

Some cool things about Beatrix:

1) She's super tall, but she doesn't slouch like a
   lot of tall girls.

2) She wears flip-flops even when it's not flip-flop weather, because her feet don't get cold until there's actual snow on the ground.

3) She just moved over the summer to Brooklyn from Manhattan and she's allowed to take the subway by herself.

"Yo," Otto and Finn said to her.

"Hi, guys," Beatrix replied, smoothing out her curly brown hair. It's sort of puffy like the top of a mushroom (both before and after her attempts to calm it down).

Beatrix wore a black cotton skirt. It was the first time I'd seen her in anything but jeans and I wondered if kids in Manhattan dressed up for each other's birthday parties. They didn't in Brooklyn and I hoped Beatrix wouldn't feel uncomfortable. Of course, she didn't look uncomfortable. Not even with Red so blatantly checking out her legs.

When he noticed me noticing, he turned red and looked away. He's often quick to blush, so maybe his name fits him better than I'd thought.

I pulled Beatrix away from the guys and over to the other side of the living room. We flopped down on the couch giggling, both of us knowing why and not needing to say.

Then the doorbell rang again and it was Sonya. When Finn let her in she looked a little panicked, standing in front of three guys. But then she noticed us and hurried over and sat down on the other side of Beatrix.

Sonya's long dark hair was braided into two neat plaits that hung down her back. She had on a tie-dyed skirt and a white long-sleeve T-shirt with a giant rainbow on it.

Both my friends had skirts on. Maybe that's what turning twelve means—dressy party clothes. I wore black pants and one of my favorite shirts—a silky baby blue button-down. My black boots had a chunky heel that made me feel tall, even though they only added an inch and a half to my height. So I didn't look like a total slob, but I wondered if maybe I should've worn a dress instead.

Lucy showed up next in cargo pants and a cute green sweater. Not hand knit or anything, but it still made me think of her scarf, so I asked her where it was.

"Oh, I didn't finish," she said.

"What scarf?" asked Beatrix.

"She's knitting this scarf for—"

"No I'm not," Lucy said, interrupting. "I changed my mind."

"Oh." I blinked. "How come?"

"No reason." She stared at me with this panicked look on her face, so I dropped the topic. But I didn't know why I had to. It was only a scarf, after all.

Suddenly I noticed Ivy standing in the entryway. She just appeared like some demon in a horror movie. Except meaner. And instead of saying something normal like "Hello," or "Sorry I've been so nasty to you for the past two years," or "I know it's pretty lame of me showing up to ruin your party," she said, "The door was open so I let myself in." And then, "Oh, hey, Beatrix. You're friends with Finn?"

"I'm friends with Maggie," Beatrix said. "Not that I have anything against Finn. I don't. I just don't really know him."

"Oh." Ivy sounded surprised, but I knew she was pretending. Our school is not that big and she's obviously seen me and Beatrix hang out together. But I let it slide, because what was I going to say? I told myself it didn't matter, even though it kind of did. I just couldn't explain why. Not even to myself.

Ivy was in pants and at first I thought, "She couldn't even bother getting dressed up for my party? How annoying!"

And then I felt silly, for the obvious reasons.

Ivy moved on, looking around all wide-eyed like she'd just landed on Mars, when she'd boarded a plane to Dallas. "Wow, this place looks exactly the same. That's so weird."

"It hasn't been that long since you were here," I said.

"It's been years," said Ivy, which I guess was true, technically.

Two years is years, plural, but I didn't want her to think I was keeping track. "Well, what's supposed to change? It's just a living room," I said.

"No need to be so sensitive, Maggs," Ivy said, making me feel dumb.

Eve and Katie trailed in a second later, and at least they had the decency to act awkward. So it was Lucy and Beatrix and Sonya and me standing across from Ivy, Katie, and Eve—an imperfect square dance of enemies.

"For Katie's birthday we got to go to Serendipity," Ivy said, apropos of nothing. "That's a really cute restaurant in Manhattan."

"It's near Bloomingdale's," Katie added.

Like I didn't know!

Okay, fine. I didn't, but so what?

Beatrix laughed. "My parents wanted me to have my ninth birthday there, but I refused because it seemed too babyish."

I shot Beatrix a grateful look and she smiled, then turned to Katie. "But I'm sure it was a really fun party."

Katie just shrugged and looked toward the guys, so everyone else did, too.

They huddled by the food, munching on pretzels and chips. They were either starving or afraid to talk to us girls or maybe both. Finn was on his third cup of soda, probably because we only get to drink it on special occasions.

I glared at my brother, silently pleading with him to rescue me from this awkwardness of his creation. And he must've gotten the message because the next thing I know, he punched Otto on the shoulder and walked over, and his friends followed.

"Hey's" and "Yo's" and "Wassup's" were exchanged, and then we all stood around wondering what to do now that we were here.

Then Ivy said, "How's it going, Otto?" all deliberate, stretching out the syllables and giggling like she'd said something dirty. Could she be more obvious?

"Hey." Otto's voice wavered, like he didn't know if he was supposed to act sweet or indifferent. Then he stared down at his shoes—black Vans with white skulls that he'd colored in with green Magic Marker.

I noticed he was wearing his Brooklyn Cyclones T-shirt. That's the minor league baseball team here. Their stadium is in Coney Island and if you sit high enough up in the bleachers you can see the ocean, which I think is more interesting than baseball but I wouldn't say so out loud. Anyway, Otto had already spilled some orange soda on his shirt—a small spot that he tried to hide with one hand, except he kept staring at it, which actually drew more attention.

A second later, Red crossed the room and plugged his iPod into my parents' stereo. "This band is coming to Southpaw next week," he said, and he cranked up the sound.

"Cool, we should go," said Otto.

Red gave him a funny look. "We already are going, doofus, remember? We got tickets last week."

"Oh yeah." Otto frowned down at his stained shirt again.

"Maybe we should go, too," Eve said sweetly. Her attempt to make Otto feel better almost made me like her.

Music filled the room in a way that none of the guests ever could, and we all started to relax. At least I did.

Then my dad came back from Two Boots—our favorite pizza place—with four pies: two with pepperoni, one all vegetable, and one with extra tomatoes and cheese. He dropped them on the table and left the room.

We attacked the food like we were starving, but probably we were all just happy to have something to do. After we got pizza I drifted over to the couch and sat down. My friends followed. The boys stayed by the food and Ivy and her friends stayed by the boys, but kind of off to the side, so it was like we were at three different parties, which I wasn't going to complain about.

"So what's the deal with those two?" asked Beatrix.

"Who?" I glanced across the room.

Eve and Otto stood next to each other, not talking. But not talking in a way that meant they liked each other. "Eve and Otto?"

"Yup." She nodded and took a large bite of pepperoni pizza. "Are they going out?"

"Not that I know of," said Lucy.

"I'll bet they will be soon," Beatrix said.

We nodded, taking Beatrix's word for it because she was the expert on this sort of thing—more so than any of us, anyway. She had two ex-boyfriends who lived on the Upper West Side.

"So, who do you like, Maggie?" asked Beatrix.

Uh-oh. Out of all my friends—and everyone else in the universe, actually—only Lucy knew about Milo. Beatrix was cool and all, but I'd only known her for a few weeks. I wasn't ready to confide in her yet, especially regarding something as monumental as my hopeless crush.

I hadn't told Sonya yet, either, even though we've been good friends since the third grade and great friends since the beginning of sixth. I can't because of the unicorns. She's really into them and I have this theory: you can love unicorns or you can love boys, but you cannot love unicorns *and* boys. It's a universal rule, like how two positive integers can never add up to a negative integer. Any alternative is mathematically impossible.

"I don't know. What about you?" I asked Beatrix.

Beatrix twirled one of her short curls around her finger as she surveyed the room. "I haven't decided yet. But no one here, I don't think."

"Me neither," Lucy said quickly, which was kind of redundant because she didn't like any boy anywhere, as she'd pointed out to me on numerous occasions.

I'll bet if Beatrix did like someone at the party, she'd have no problem making a move. She's bold like that. Meanwhile, I couldn't talk about anything real because I was scared Ivy would overhear and think I sounded dumb.

I glanced across the room, wishing she'd just disappear. And that's when I realized she had.

"Where is she?" I asked.

"Who?" asked Sonya, chewing on the end of her braid.

"Ivy," Lucy replied. "Whenever Maggie says 'she' like it's a dirty word, she's talking about Ivy."

"That's not true," I said. Then I thought about it for a second. "Is it?"

Lucy nodded.

"Maybe she's in the bathroom?" Sonya guessed.

Beatrix shrugged. "Or maybe she got bored and left early."

"I wish," I said, and then had this cold flash of panic. Was Beatrix implying that my party was boring?

Just then Finn came over and said, "Time for the poker tournament."

"Cool!" said Beatrix.

"Can I be on your team?" asked Lucy.

"I don't know how to play," said Sonya.

"I'll teach you. It's easy," Finn said, then smiled at Lucy. "You, too. There are no teams."

"Oh, I know," said Lucy, tucking her hair behind her ears and smiling down at her lap. "I was just kidding."

He turned to me. "I'll get the cards if you get the chips. They're in my desk—the drawer on the left."

"Okay, be right back," I called to my friends as I turned around and headed out.

As soon as I walked through my bedroom door I jumped, totally shocked.

I wasn't expecting to see Ivy standing by the fake fireplace.

Meanwhile, she probably wasn't expecting to see anyone.

Not when she had my cigar box in one hand . . . and all my dog-walking money in the other.

Chapter 11

. . .

Ivy and I used to do everything together: Music and ballet when we were little. Fencing and T-ball when we got older. Scrapbook making, modern dance, quilting, origami . . . All these activities our parents signed us up for. Some fun. Some dumb.

I even helped her pick out Kermit—the most adorable black-and-white Labrador Dalmatian mutt you've ever seen. We were nine then and Ivy said he could be my dog, too.

We walked him every day after school, taking turns holding his leash.

I helped her give Kermit his first bath—a wet, soapy disaster.

Helped her carry home his first big bag of dog food from Acme Pet Food (before we found out they delivered for free).

He really felt like my dog.

Just like Ivy really felt almost like a sister.

Then Eve O'Sullivan's parents had twin boys. They all moved to Brooklyn and everything changed.

At first it was small stuff: Eve and Ivy giggled over stuff that wasn't even funny. They had matching retro rainbow flip-flops and thought it proved they were destined to be friends. More likely it meant that Urban Outfitters had a sale on flip-flops, but when I pointed this out they accused me of being jealous.

One day the two of them set up a lemonade stand outside Ivy's building.

I asked if I could help out. They said there wasn't room. And that was the beginning of the end.

The Ivy I knew disappeared—morphed into a different person: a girl who had perfect hair and actually thought that made her better than everyone else.

A girl who wore eye shadow in the sixth grade and real lipstick, not just tinted gloss.

A girl whose socks always matched her shirts, which coordinated with her belts.

A girl who made fun of those who didn't get their ears pierced because maybe they were afraid of needles.

A girl who doled out dirty looks the way she used to pass out sticks of gum.

In short, Ivy turned into someone I didn't even know. Someone I no longer even liked. And yet, I still missed her.

But how can you miss someone who doesn't even exist anymore? Two years should have been enough time for me to get over it and move on. And I had, for the most part.

I already knew that Ivy was a lot of things—backstabbing; gossipy; and, okay, even pretty mean. But I never knew she was a thief, too.

Yet here she was, taking my stuff.

"Steal from me much?"

Ivy screamed and jumped what seemed like a mile.

"You scared me," she yelled, all accusing—like I was supposed to feel bad.

"Should I apologize for getting in the way of your robbery?"

"It's not like that," Ivy cried. And that's when I noticed her glassy red eyes. She swiped her shiny tears from her face with the back of her hand.

But were they real? I couldn't tell. There was a time when I'd have given her the benefit of the doubt. Those days were long gone.

"I can explain," she said, staring down at the cash in her hand like she didn't know how it got there.

I walked across the room and grabbed my box back.

"I can't believe you still have that," said Ivy.

It's not that I'm so sentimental. I swear I didn't keep the cigar box because I was pining over our lost friendship. Rather, the box was one of the coolest gifts anyone had ever given me. It's faded red with a map of the world inside. Musty smelling like it had an exciting history. We used to hide stuff in it when we played Pirates, an elaborate treasure-hunting game we made up. But that was a long time ago.

"It's just a stupid box," I said, opening the lid and checking to see that the keys and all my other dog-walking things were still there.

"I don't need any of that junk," Ivy said. "And I wasn't going to take all of your cash."

"Oh, sorry for the confusion. I should've known you were only going to steal *a little* from me. You know, since it's my birthday and all." I held out my hand and she gave up the stack of bills. I counted it in front of her—figuring it was all there but knowing it would annoy her.

"I only need some of it and I can explain."

I was so angry I was shaking. "It looks pretty obvious to me, Ivy. First you crash my party and then you try to steal from me? Like it isn't enough to torture me at school every day? You have to come to my house and ruin my weekends, too?"

"I don't torture you," she said. "And the money is for Kermit."

"You're stealing money for your dog?" I asked. "Well, that certainly clears things up. What is it, credit card debt? Poor guy. I didn't realize he was such a big spender."

"Don't be like this, Maggie. I'm serious. Kermit's in trouble."

Ivy pulled a small blue note card from her back pocket and handed it to me. "I wanted to tell you, but I figured this would be easier. And for the record, I was going to pay you back."

I grabbed the note. The printing was so neat it almost looked typed.

Want to see Kermit again? Bring $100 in an
unmarked envelope to the dog beach in Prospect
Park tomorrow at noon. Tape it to the nearest
park bench and walk away. Make sure you come
alone.

"I don't get it," I said.

"Someone stole Kermit and they're holding him for ransom," she said. "And no one else knows—not even Katie or Eve and especially not my parents, so you have to promise me you'll keep quiet."

I glanced at her skeptically. "Is this a joke?"

"No, it's serious." The way her voice broke, the way her whole posture seemed off—anxious, really—made me believe her. "And you can't tell anyone."

"I'm not promising a thing," I said. "But you'd still better explain."

"Fine." Ivy huffed out a small breath in angry defeat. "My parents are in England for two weeks, visiting my grandma because she's sick, and they left me with my other grandma and she was out with her bridge club, so I took Kermit to a stoop sale where I found this very cool top and then I saw a bunch of Diane von Furstenberg wrap dresses in the window at Beacon's Closet and—" Ivy paused and looked me up and down. "Beacon's Closet is on Fifth Avenue. They sell—"

"I know what Beacon's Closet is."

"Just checking." She held up her hands, all fake innocent.

Ivy's always been way into old clothes and she's got this whole reverse-snobbery attitude about it. She prides herself on finding cool vintage stuff at used-clothing stores and stoop sales and even online. And it is a skill. It's just, I don't know why she thinks this makes her better than other people. Everyone has something they're good at. And for me, it's not fashion. But so what? "I'm not stupid."

"I know. I'm just telling you. It was an emergency. The dress display was adorable, but I had Kermit, so—"

I cut her off. "Did you wash your hands really well after you cleaned up after him?"

"Maggie!"

"I'm just saying. Dogs carry all types of icky diseases." I did my best imitation of her. I couldn't help myself.

"Okay, fine." She rolled her eyes. "I'm sorry, okay? It was just a joke."

"Well, you forgot to make it funny."

"Oh, who cares? No one heard."

"Everyone heard!"

"Everyone?" She raised her eyebrows, all condescending. "I seriously doubt that."

"Everyone in the Pizza Den. Milo, for instance." I didn't want to harp on this, but his name just slipped out.

"Well, at least no one good heard."

"What's that supposed to mean?"

"Milo's a dork. He doesn't count."

I started to object but stopped myself. Milo was so much more than a dork, but maybe it was better if Ivy thought of him that way. There'd be less competition. Plus, I didn't want her knowing I liked him.

"Wait a second." Ivy smiled like she could read my mind. "You like him."

"Who?"

"Milo. It's obvious." She clapped and said, "Ha! That's so typical."

"I don't like him," I said, but I couldn't meet her gaze. "And what do you mean by typical?"

"Just that he's totally your type—tall, skinny, floppy-haired. All quiet so you never know what he's thinking. I guess he's not hideous, but he definitely needs a ward-robe update. Have you noticed that sweater he always wears? The one with the big hole?"

"Tell me more about Kermit. What time did you lose him?"

"What?" she asked. "Oh yeah. I tied him up at around three-thirty and he was gone by a quarter to four."

"How did you do it?"

"What do you mean?"

"What kind of knot?"

"I don't know. Square? You know I was always bad at knots in Girl Scouts." Ivy grinned and I had to smile back. We'd both dropped out of Girl Scouts in the third grade—right before we got our rope-tying badges—because Ivy claimed it was a fascist organization. I didn't know what that meant at the time, but it sounded cool, so I kept saying it, too, and eventually our parents got sick of hearing us complain and signed us up for a pottery class instead.

"Anyway, it was only a few minutes," Ivy said.

"Before you said fifteen."

Ivy cringed guiltily. "Okay, I don't know *exactly* how long it was. I guess I sort of lost track."

I shook my head. "I can't believe you left him on the street."

"Do you know how bad I feel? And I already told you it was an emergency . . ."

"A shopping emergency?"

"Yes!" Ivy screamed. "I abandoned my dog so I could shop. I'm a horrible person! I can't even walk by Beacon's Closet without feeling sick."

"Did you see anything suspicious? Or anyone? Do you think someone followed you, maybe? Can you think of anyone who might do this?"

"Like, does Kermit have any enemies?" she asked. "He's a dog!"

"I know. I'm just asking. Tell me what happened again. From the beginning this time."

Ivy took a deep breath and huffed. "Fine. So I tied Kermit to a parking meter directly in front of the store, where I'd be able to see him through the window the whole time. Then I went inside and—"

"If you could see him the whole time, how did he get dognapped?"

Ivy frowned. "I could see him when I was looking at dresses, but the sunglasses display case is in the back."

I groaned.

"It's not my fault," said Ivy. "I made one tiny mistake. In one moment, I had the perfect dress for the fall dance. And in the next, my dog vanished."

"That's horrible," I said. I meant it, too. And in the back of my mind, I also marveled at how she already had an outfit for the dance, which was a whole month away. I had no idea if I was even going. And she'd already figured out what to wear?

I wondered if she had a date. Then I got annoyed with myself for caring.

Meanwhile, Ivy sat cross-legged on my floor, in tears. She seemed so upset I had to believe her.

I handed her a tissue. She blew her nose, loudly, and went on. "I found this cop a block over and I tried to tell him, but he didn't believe me. I think he thought it was a joke. The way he looked at me—like I was wasting his time. It was awful. And I tried calling the police later on, but they said that dognapping is not a nine-one-one type of emergency and could they please speak to my parents. So I said no and hung up fast. And now Kermit's gone and my parents will be home in ten days and they'll never forgive me."

"You didn't tell your grandma?" I asked.

"No. She's kind of forgetful and she doesn't like dogs. I'm supposed to keep Kermit away from her whenever she's at the house, so I don't think she's even noticed that he's missing."

I hadn't seen Ivy this upset since we got grounded for throwing water balloons out her window when we were in third grade. (And to be fair, that had been my idea.)

"But it's not your fault," I said.

"It kind of is. My parents warned me not to tie up Kermit. And they think I buy too many clothes. So this is the ultimate. I didn't know what to do until I remembered what you said about dog walking yesterday. My cousin used to walk dogs when he was in law school and he said it was the best job he ever had. Paid well, too. So I figured you had the cash. I mean, obviously you're not spending money on clothes." She looked me up and down.

"It's amazing how you can ask me for help *and* be insulting at the very same time."

"It's a gift." Ivy shrugged. "But whatever. I'm only stating a fact and you know I'll pay you back. I'm supposed to babysit next Friday and for three Saturday nights in a row. You'll have the money in no time."

Ivy stared at me, desperate. And as much as I wanted to say forget it, I thought of Kermit. One of my favorite dogs in the world, and the one with the saddest puppyhood I'd ever known.

He'd been found in an abandoned building when he was days old. His mom was gone and his whole litter was alone. Two had died by the time the shelter found them. And once we finally convinced Ivy's parents that they must—absolutely had to—adopt one of the puppies, Kermit was the only one left. He had black-and-white shaggy fur and spots. The skinniest little body you've ever seen—we could see his ribs, even. Huge, fat paws that told us he'd grow up to be enormous. And he did. One time, this kid on the street mistook him for a donkey.

I couldn't believe he was gone.

Despite what Ivy did and despite the girl she'd become, I had to help Kermit. A hundred dollars was a lot of money, but I had it. No way could I refuse.

Still, reading the note gave me the chills. What kind of person would do something like this? No one I wanted to meet.

"I don't think you should go alone," I found myself saying.

Ivy's eyebrows shot up. "But I have to. The note says—"

"I know what the note says, but think about it. It could be dangerous. What if he or she tries to kidnap *you*? Are you sure you can't tell your parents?"

She shook her head. "There's no way."

"Well, what about my parents? They'd help, I bet."

"No, they'll just invoke the parent code and call my parents. You can't say a word." Ivy's cold blue eyes bore into me, letting me know she meant business. She spoke carefully, urgently. "I need to get Kermit back and I need to listen to this person's instructions. So are you going to help me or what?"

I looked down at the note and then up at Ivy.

I didn't answer right away, but I knew not to argue.

Once Ivy made up her mind, there was no going back.

Chapter 12

. . .

Some pigeons can fly at speeds of up to a hundred miles an hour. Peregrine falcons move twice as fast. And hummingbirds need to eat every ten minutes.

Who cares? I asked myself the very same thing, back when my dad made me watch his National Geographic documentary on bird-watching in New York City. But now I'm grateful for these seemingly useless facts because they'll provide me with the perfect cover.

On Sunday, I put on my softest jeans, my scuffed blue Pumas, and one of Finn's old shirts (green, long-sleeved, and slightly baggy). I dumped my schoolbooks out of my backpack and filled it with some dog-walking supplies instead: spare leash, biscuits, water, and bowl. I slipped my camera into my back pocket and slung my dad's binoculars around my neck to complete the disguise.

Looking like a girl going after an evil dognapper

was too dangerous, which is why I transformed myself into Maggie Brooklyn, Bird-Watcher.

I even looked up a bunch of bird facts in case I met another bird-watcher and had to act the part. I was ready.

At least I would be once I ate breakfast.

"Where are you off to?" my mom asked. She was up early, drinking coffee and paying bills at the kitchen table.

"The park," I said as innocently as possible.

She looked at me from over the tops of her reading glasses. "By yourself?"

She seemed to know I was up to something, and I had no reason to lie. "Actually, I'm meeting up with Ivy."

I took an English muffin out of the bread box, sliced it open, and put it in the toaster. Even though my back was to her, I could feel Mom's extra wide smile radiate across the room.

"Why do you look like you're auditioning for a toothpaste commercial?" I asked, turning around.

"I'm just so happy that you and Ivy have put this silly feud behind you."

"Feud?" I asked. "Whoever said we were in the middle of a feud?"

"Well, whatever it was, I'm glad it's over. It was so nice seeing you two talk at your party."

"You weren't supposed to be watching," I reminded her.

"Right," said Mom. "But when Finn tried to get that game of Five-Card Stud going with actual money, I had to intervene."

"The stakes were low. We were only playing for quarters."

"Gambling is gambling," said Mom. "But that doesn't matter. Have a great time today."

"Will do," I called on my way out.

Today was all about rescuing Kermit. If it made my mom feel better to think Ivy and I were friends again, then fine. There was no harm in keeping her clueless. In fact, it made things easier. Fewer questions that way.

I polished off breakfast on my way to Beacon's Closet. When I got there I found Ivy sitting on a bench in front of the coffee place next door.

"What are you wearing?" she asked as soon as she noticed me.

"It's my disguise," I told her, which should've been obvious.

"You're dressed as a dork?" she asked with a laugh. "Not much of a disguise."

"For someone asking for so many favors, you sure are rude."

Ivy shrugged. "I'm only being honest."

"I'm dressed as a bird-watcher," I said, holding up the binoculars. "And I wore sneakers in case there's a chase. Something you maybe should've thought of." I stared pointedly at her platform boots.

I knew I had her, but she still shrugged and said, "Dork, bird-watcher. Same thing." All dismissive.

"Do you want my help or not?"

"I'm not sure," said Ivy. "They said to come alone."

"Right. We've been over this and we agreed it would be a bad idea to—"

"*You* agreed and that was last night. I've been thinking, the park's a public place, and it's always packed on weekends. I mean, what could happen in broad daylight?"

"That's how Kermit got stolen in the first place," I reminded her. "Plus, last year someone snatched my mom's purse in the middle of the afternoon, and they never even caught the guy."

Ivy sighed heavily. "Fine. It's your money, so I guess you call the shots."

"It's not like that," I said. "I just think we need to figure out who's behind the dognapping. Because what if they do this again?"

"I'd never leave Kermit alone twice. If I get him back, I won't let him out of my sight."

"I mean, what if they do this to other dogs?" I said.

"Oh." Ivy thought for a moment, her narrow eyebrows scrunched together. "Okay, that makes sense. Did you bring the cash?"

I pulled a small white envelope from my back pocket and handed it to Ivy. "Here."

She stood, dusted off the back of her jeans, and inspected it. The envelope was unmarked, as specified, and bulky with my hundred dollars, cash. (Mostly old bills—I'd saved Cassie's for myself.)

"It's all there," I said. "Count it if you want."

"I trust you."

We walked to the park in silence—six long blocks. Ivy's boots clicked against the sidewalk, fast and annoyed.

One thing about Ivy: she wasn't going to pretend to like me just because I was doing her this favor—waking up extra early on a Sunday and lending her most of my dog-walking money—when she wasn't even my friend anymore.

If anything, she acted like she resented me more than ever. Which annoyed me and made me wonder why I'd agreed to help in the first place.

But I tried to look for the positives: like, maybe I should be refreshed by her honesty?

It wasn't easy.

"So you know what you're supposed to do?" I asked once we were across the street from the park.

"Tape the cash to the park bench and walk away," said Ivy. "Meanwhile, you'll be watching from your hiding place. And when you yell 'Kermit,' I turn around and we corner the dognapper and scream for help."

I nodded. "Yup. That's it."

"But what if it doesn't work?"

"How can it not work?"

Ivy frowned. "It's just so simple."

"Simple plans are the best," I assured her.

She narrowed her eyes at me, suspicious. "Says who?"

"Says me. Don't worry so much." I checked my watch. "It's almost time. We shouldn't be talking. They might be watching now."

Ivy looked around. "You think?" She sounded a little panicked, which made me feel better. At least she was taking this seriously.

"I don't know. I hope not. You go in first and I'll hang back."

"Okay." Ivy waited for the light to change and crossed the street, walking stiffly between the panther statues.

I followed a couple of minutes later.

Once I got to the park, I stopped and pretended to admire some birdlife, but unfortunately all I could see at the moment were some pigeons picking at a stale-looking hot-dog bun.

Still, I squinted at them through my binoculars, pulled out my notepad, and pretended to write down my observations.

Then I moved on, heading toward the designated park bench, but not directly.

Once I got within fifty feet or so, I ducked behind a tree, crouched down, and stared at the bench through my binoculars.

The envelope was there and Ivy had just walked away, looking about as awkward as I felt.

Ivy was right. It did seem dorky coming to the park with gigantic binoculars.

I hoped I didn't run into anyone I knew. And right as I was having that thought—as if I'd conjured up my biggest fear—I heard a familiar voice speaking from behind me.

"You again?"

I spun around and found myself face-to-face with the dark-haired dog walker. This time she had only one client with her—a chubby basset hound with droopy, bloodshot eyes.

"Spying on the competition?" she asked.

So much for being inconspicuous. Then I realized something: if it looked like I was in conversation with the crazy dog-walker lady, Kermit's dognapper wouldn't know I was watching him or her.

"Hi, I'm Maggie." I held out my hand and tried to be as friendly as possible. "I never did catch your name."

"It's Jane," she said with a scowl. "What are you doing here?"

"Well, not that it's any of your business," I said as I held up my binoculars, "but I happen to be an avid bird-watcher."

"You have time for hobbies? It must be nice. I'm too busy working and worrying about my business. I lost another client yesterday."

"Lost?" I gulped, thinking about the chocolate Lab's close brush with death.

"Yeah, it seems that Daphne's parents found a cheaper dog walker."

"Daphne?" I glanced back at the envelope, wanting to keep the conversation short but knowing I couldn't let Jane see what I was up to.

I edged away and sat down on the nearest bench. Unfortunately, she joined me. "Are you *sure* you don't know her?"

"I don't. Seriously—I don't have any new dogs. I'm not even looking for any new dogs. I'm busy enough. What with my bird-watching hobby." I held up my binoculars to remind her. "Did you know that over thirty-six types of warblers have been spotted in this park?"

Jane huffed, thoroughly unimpressed with my bird factoid.

"I've only seen two myself, but this is new for me." I spoke as earnestly as possible, feeling more like someone pretending to be a dork than an actual dork. A subtle but necessary distinction.

"So you're still going with the 'innocent kid' act?" she asked.

"Oh, it's no act. I'm *barely* twelve, and I've never stolen anything in my life. Never broken and entered. Never shoplifted—not even a piece of candy. I've never trespassed, as far as I know. I'm a Girl Scout. Metaphorically speaking, of course. I used to be a Girl Scout for real, but that was a long time ago and I always hated the uniform. The cookies were good. Especially the Thin—"

"Do you have a point?" Jane snapped.

"Absolutely. I'm not only innocent, I'm the definition of innocence. Look up innocent on Wikipedia; you'll see my smiling face." Okay, maybe I got carried away, but I really wanted to be clear with her.

"I have to work weekends now, just to stay competitive," Jane said, like she didn't even hear me.

She really had a one-track mind. In this woman's imagination, we were in some major competition and I didn't know how to convince her otherwise.

"Look, I'm glad you stopped by to say hello. But I'm kind of busy right now." I smiled, turned around, and raised my binoculars to my face.

Meanwhile, Jane still sat next to me, fuming. "Know

what, Maggie? You're treating this like a joke, but there's nothing funny about this situation and you'd better watch your back."

"Okay," I said. "But right now I'd like to get back to watching birds." I spotted the right bench and adjusted the binoculars.

"Do whatever you want to do," said Jane. "But don't say you weren't warned."

"Warned?" I tore my gaze from the bench, alarmed. "What's that supposed to mean?"

Jane didn't answer. She couldn't because she'd already stormed off, pulling that poor basset hound along behind her.

By the time I turned back to the dog beach, I couldn't find the right bench. I thought it was the third from the end, but when I focused on it, I couldn't see an envelope. And it wasn't on the next one, either.

"Where were you?" I heard someone ask.

I spun around, figuring from the angry tone that Jane had returned. But it was only Ivy. An extremely irate Ivy.

"What?" I asked.

"Who was it? Where are they?"

Oh no. I felt a slow, sinking feeling in the pit of my stomach. "You mean it already happened?" I asked. "They took the envelope?"

"Of course they took it!" Ivy yelled.

"Then where's Kermit?" I asked.

"Don't know," said Ivy.

"But I only looked away for a second . . ."

"And that's all it took!"

We both glanced toward the bench, and I suddenly spotted another small blue note card. We ran over. I got there first and pulled it loose. Then Ivy snatched it from me before I had time to read it.

" 'I said to come alone,' " Ivy read. She angrily waved the card in my face. "I can't believe I was so stupid!"

"This isn't your fault," I said.

"I know that!" screamed Ivy. "I mean I shouldn't have trusted you. *That* was my big mistake."

"I'm so sorry." It was all I could manage to say, what with the gigantic lump invading my throat.

"You said you knew what you were doing!" Ivy yelled.

My whole body felt heavy with dread. Like I'd had rocks for breakfast instead of that slightly stale English muffin. "Okay, I never said that exactly."

"You said you'd help, but actually you made things a thousand times worse! Which is so typical."

"What's that supposed to mean?"

"Nothing." Ivy pouted.

"It's not over. We can still find him."

"How?" asked Ivy. "It's impossible. And you wonder why I don't hang out with you anymore!"

"But—" I didn't finish my sentence. For one thing, I didn't know how to. But more importantly, Ivy had run away.

I chased her. Which wasn't easy because my binoculars bounced up and down against my chest and my backpack shifted with each step. I tried holding the binoculars with one hand, but that made running harder.

And it turned out I was wrong about the boots. They didn't slow Ivy down at all. I moved as fast as I could, but she was faster, darting away from the dog beach, zipping past the baseball fields, and tearing across the Long Meadow.

People flew kites, picnicked in the last of the sunny weather, tossed Frisbees. No one looked twice as Ivy tore by—determined, a girl on a mission. But where was she going?

I soon found out.

Suddenly she ran into the middle of one of the soccer games on the Great Lawn. A bunch of guys, half in red shirts and half in blue shirts, were playing. They looked about our age, maybe a bit older, but I didn't recognize any of them, which meant they probably went to one of the private schools nearby.

I figured it was an accident, busting up their game, but what Ivy did next was completely deliberate.

Deliberate and shocking.

Ivy stole the game ball. Kicked it away, then picked it up and held it over her head.

The guys who were chasing the ball stopped short. They looked at her and then at one another and then back at her.

A short guy with blond hair and braces said, "Huh?"

Another player asked, "What's going on?"

Soon their confusion melted into anger.

Obviously they thought this girl was disturbed, and I couldn't say I blamed them. I was starting to wonder the same thing.

"Um, can you give that back?" asked another guy.

Ivy shook her head so hard her ponytail came loose. "Forget it," she yelled, hugging the ball tight against her chest in an iron death grip. "I'm not letting go until you tell me where Kermit is."

Chapter 13

◆ ◆ ◆

All the soccer players shifted back to their original state—bewilderment. And they weren't the only ones.

"She's asking for Kermit?" one asked.

"He's my dog." Ivy sniffed. "But you know that."

"I thought Kermit was a frog," another guy said. (The only one in shorts rather than sweatpants.)

"Dude, she's not talking about the Muppet," said a tall, spiky-haired one.

"Obviously," Ivy grumbled.

The players looked at each other. Some concerned, some annoyed. All completely lost.

"Um, Ivy?" I asked, taking a step toward her.

She whipped around and shot me a look of death. "Don't even try and speak to me now, Maggie."

I froze, scared to move closer.

A few of the guys huddled together and whispered

for a minute or so. Then the one with braces headed toward Ivy.

"You're the girl from last Saturday? With the big dog?" He held out his hands, a pantomime of Kermit's girth.

"Yes," snapped Ivy. "Obviously I'm that girl. So stop acting all innocent and tell me where Kermit is."

"You think we took him?" The guy seemed thoroughly—and legitimately—confused.

Ivy blinked and loosened her grip on the soccer ball ever so slightly. "Of course you took him."

"Um, no." He shook his head.

I didn't know what Ivy was doing but one thing was clear: these guys didn't, either. She seemed so convinced, but my gut told me that none of them stole her dog.

And I have a pretty smart gut. I think that's how I'm always able to find Isabel's missing stuff. I just wished it could have told me who took Kermit. And where we could find him. And how to talk to Milo. And why he acted so weird in the park the other day. But I suppose that's asking too much. After all, every gut has its limits.

"Seriously, Ivy. These guys don't know what you're talking about." I spoke firmly but gently, knowing the subject was sensitive.

And the longer Ivy stood there, the more the truth seemed to sink in.

"But if you didn't, then who did?" she cried.

I put my hand on her arm.

When Ivy glanced at me, I saw so much pain swimming around in her eyes, my own heart felt splintered.

Splintered but still confused.

"Um, can you tell me what's going on? Why you think these guys have Kermit? And how you even know them?"

"From last Saturday," Ivy said. "I was playing fetch with Kermit, and instead of retrieving his Frisbee, he fetched their soccer ball."

"And they were mad?" I asked.

She nodded. "They said it was a high-stakes match."

"But Kermit's just a dog. It's not his fault."

"No, they were mad at me," said Ivy. "For playing so close and for not being able to control my dog. It took, like, almost five minutes to get back their ball."

"That's not so long."

"I know, but Kermit punctured it in two places. It was totally flat. And no one had a spare ball, so we ruined their whole game."

"Why didn't you tell me?" I asked.

"I didn't think it mattered. I figured once they got the money they'd return Kermit. The thing is, they wanted me to pay for the ball on the spot, but I refused."

"Why?" I asked.

"I didn't have any cash on me," Ivy said, all defensive like it should've been obvious. "And that blond guy with braces? He's the one who finally caught Kermit, and when he did, he wrestled him to the ground and Kermit whimpered and the whole thing was awful. So I got mad and I yelled at him."

Ivy twisted up her mouth. A classic stubborn Ivy move. She didn't have to explain further. I could figure out what had happened on my own. Ivy gave them attitude. Something she does all the time. And those guys didn't just get mad. They got even. That's what she thought, anyway.

Except she was wrong. They didn't steal Kermit. The soccer players were innocent. I was sure of it.

But since I was dealing with Ivy, I couldn't just come out and tell her that she was mistaken.

"Do you really think they'd kidnap Kermit?" I asked.

Ivy bit her bottom lip. "You should've seen how mad they were."

"Still . . ."

"And who else would take him?"

I looked toward the group of guys. They didn't seem like the dognapping type. In fact, I thought they were being pretty patient, given the circumstances. I tried to reason with her. "If they were holding Kermit for ransom, they'd have gotten what they wanted by now.

More, even. No soccer ball costs a hundred dollars, I don't think. So they'd have returned him, right?"

"Then how can you explain what happened to Kermit?"

"I can't," I answered honestly. "But we'll figure it out."

"Really? You think? Because you already screwed up once."

"We'll find Kermit. I know we will. Just give the ball back, okay?"

After giving it a bit of thought, Ivy said, "Fine." And she handed over the ball, mumbling, "Sorry."

"Let's head back to the bench. Maybe we can find some clues."

Ivy scoffed. "Who are you, Nancy Drew?"

"Not a very good one," I said.

"Obviously," said Ivy, but she followed me anyway.

"What are we looking for?" she asked once we arrived back at the bench, which luckily was still empty.

"Don't know. Suspicious-looking footprints, perhaps?" I looked down at the surrounding dirt, loosely packed and perfect for capturing footprints. So perfect there were traces of them everywhere.

"How does a suspicious footprint distinguish itself from a regular old print?" asked Ivy.

"Um . . ." I couldn't really answer.

Ivy grew impatient. "Well, there are a gazillion footprints here."

I hated to admit it, but she was right. It was beautiful out and everyone was in the park. Which meant there was no way of knowing which footprints belonged to the dognapper. No evidence for us to gather and nothing left to do.

"Are you sure we can't go to the police?" I asked.

"And do what?" said Ivy. "Tell them I taped a hundred dollars to a park bench and someone took it? What kind of crime is that?"

"If you show them the note—"

"I can't do that." Ivy turned around and headed toward the park exit.

"Wait!" I called, following her.

Ivy looked over her shoulder. "Forget it. It's over. Kermit is gone."

"Maybe they'll get in touch with you again." I ran to catch up with her. "Kermit has tags with your phone number, right?"

Ivy nodded.

"So maybe they'll call and ask for more money."

"I don't have any more money."

"Well, I do. And I'll give them whatever they want, as long as they bring Kermit back safe."

"Thanks." Ivy frowned but not in an angry way. More like she was thinking. Sort of like the Ivy I used to know. And I could tell she appreciated my offer. At least for a second. But then she shifted back to her snappish self. The new Ivy. The one I didn't know and didn't love. "I can't believe the dognapper got away when you were busy blabbing to Plain Jane."

I stopped short and grabbed Ivy's arm. "Wait, you mean Jane the dog walker? You know her?"

"Duh," said Ivy. "She used to walk Kermit."

I raised my eyebrows. "Used to?"

"Yeah, until my parents had to fire her."

"When was that?"

"About a month ago."

"Why? What happened?"

"What didn't happen?" Ivy replied. "She was totally incompetent. First she lost our keys. Then she forgot to lock the door behind her, and then she made the ulti-mate mistake: she mixed up Kermit with some other dog and we came home one night to some strange-looking mutt chewing up our living room couch."

"Wow, she really is a lousy dog walker."

"No kidding. We're lucky we got Kermit back in one piece," said Ivy.

"Maybe," I said carefully. "Or maybe you guys were unlucky to hire Jane in the first place. Way unlucky."

Ivy stopped in her tracks. "Wait, you think Jane stole Kermit?"

"It's just a theory . . ."

"But she was talking to you when the money was taken. It couldn't have been her."

"Unless she wasn't acting alone."

"You think?"

I shrugged. "Who knows? I'm going to call Parminder."

"Who?"

"Parminder Patel. Our old teacher. I walk her dog, Milo, and this other dog in her building, Bean. Jane used to walk them both and that's how I met her in the first place. She got mad and accused me of stealing her clients."

"Did you?" asked Ivy.

"Of course not. Parminder hired me out of the blue. I'd never even heard of Jane until I ran into her last week. And Parminder must have had a good reason for firing her. Maybe if I knew what it was, we could figure this out."

"But why would Jane steal Kermit?"

"Maybe for revenge?" I guessed. "She's pretty hostile. Maybe she's trying to teach your family a lesson. Or perhaps she just found a creative way to make back the money she wasn't earning, now that her client list is shrinking."

"That's so evil!"

"No kidding."

We were out of the park and walking down Third Street when I noticed something taped to a nearby streetlamp. A yellow flyer with a picture of a dog on it.

HAVE YOU SEEN LASSIE? it read in bold black type.

The description was printed below it in slightly smaller letters:

Sixty-pound female collie, white and brown, missing since Sunday. Last seen in Prospect Park, near the dog beach. If found, please call (718) 555-7436. Reward.

The sight of it made me queasy.

Ivy noticed me staring and asked, "You don't think Jane took *that* dog, too?"

"Don't know. It's a weird coincidence." I unzipped my backpack, pulled out a pen, and copied down the number in my notebook.

"What are you doing?"

"I'm going to call them. See if they know Jane or someone else at Dial-A-Walker."

"But this dog disappeared."

"Actually, we don't know that. The sign only says she's missing."

"Why wouldn't they just say dognapped?" asked Ivy.

I shrugged. "Dunno. Maybe they don't want to make the dognapper angry? But I think they're on to something. We should make signs for Kermit—plaster the neighborhood. Someone must've seen something. Kermit is gigantic. Distinctive looking, too."

"We can't do that," said Ivy.

"Why not?"

"First of all, my grandmother might see."

"But she hasn't even noticed he's missing."

"And I don't want to advertise the fact!" said Ivy. "Plus, Kermit's not missing. He's been dognapped. And we've already upset whoever is behind this. I don't want to make him or her mad all over again. Who knows what they'll do to the poor guy?"

"Okay, that's a good point," I said, and then I shivered as something even creepier occurred to me. Something I didn't want to mention to Ivy because it was too upsetting to say out loud.

If Jane had kidnapped Kermit, were Milo and Bean next?

Chapter 14

• • •

I didn't want to jump to any conclusions or accuse an innocent person. But I definitely needed to investigate things further. And Jane was my only lead. Luckily I knew of two people who might have information on her.

So after Ivy and I parted ways, I ran home and called Parminder. No one answered so I left a message.

When I tried Cassie I got her voicemail, too. *"Bean and I are off on a hike. Leave a message for us after the beep!"* was recorded in a chipper voice, with Bean barking in the background. As tempted as I was to ask how many people called to speak with her dog, I refrained and merely requested that she call me back.

And since I had the phone in my hand, I also called the number from the "Missing Lassie" flyer. It rang and rang without ever going to voicemail.

Next I went to my laptop and Googled "Dial-A-Walker, Brooklyn." Nothing came up. I tried "Brooklyn Dog

Walker" and found tons of companies: City Dog Sitters, Mobile Mutts, Tails on the Town, Fetch Your Pet, and others. None of the companies was called Dial-A-Walker. It wasn't listed when I called information, either.

I wondered if the place where Jane worked even existed. She could've made it up. But her sweatshirt had the company name embroidered on it. Why would she go to the trouble?

Maybe the company was just starting out and didn't yet have a Web site. Perhaps Jane was the only employee.

But what if dog walking was merely her cover? And Jane's true motivation revolved around gaining access to neighborhood dogs so she could steal them?

What if that sweatshirt was part of her brilliant disguise?

My insides fluttered with panic just thinking about the possibilities.

I pulled out a notebook to write down clues, but before I even found a pen, my mom poked her head into my room. "Finn left for art class ten minutes ago. Shouldn't you be going, too?" she asked.

"Oh yeah. Sorry, I totally spaced." I slipped my notebook under my pillow.

"Dad and I are heading to IKEA to look for a new living room couch later on. Want to come?" she asked.

"Um, no thanks. But can you bring back some Swedish meatballs for dinner?"

"They're already on the list."

"Cool." I gathered my things and then hurried to the museum.

I walked in five minutes late. Finn and the other students were already working. This month we were focused on still lifes and today we had to paint a bunch of plump red grapes, shiny red apples, and green pears in a large wooden bowl.

There is nothing more frustrating than being stuck inside painting a bowl of fruit when you are trying to track down a missing dog.

The two-hour class felt more like a ten-hour session in boredom and pointlessness. As soon as we were dismissed, I bolted home and called Ivy. "Any word from the dognapper?" I asked as soon as she answered. Instead of hello, even.

"Nope," she replied.

"And you're sure Kermit's tags have your home number?"

"Of course," said Ivy.

"Not your mom's or dad's cell phones?"

"Trust me—if my parents heard from the dognapper, they'd be on the first plane home and I'd know about it."

"Okay, good point."

"Not that the dognapper is even going to call," said Ivy.

"Don't say that. You've gotta stay positive."

"Kind of hard, since Kermit's been missing for four days now. Did you talk to Ms. Patel or that other lady?"

"You mean Cassie? They're not home but I left them both messages. Has your grandma noticed that Kermit is missing?"

"Not yet," said Ivy.

"Well, that's a good thing," I said. "And don't worry. The dognapper will get in touch."

"How can you be so sure?"

I wasn't sure. I was hopeful—two very different things. But I didn't say so. "We're going to find Kermit," I promised before hanging up.

Finn had gone to Otto's right from the museum and my parents were still out furniture shopping, which meant the house was quiet. Too quiet—it made me antsy.

I could've gone to Lucy's. I saw that she'd called while I was out. But I'd promised Ivy I wouldn't say a word about Kermit's dognapping, and the best way to keep secrets from anyone was to avoid them. This I knew.

So I pulled out my notebook and tried, once more, to write down clues. Unfortunately, nothing came to me.

I stared at my phone for a while, willing it to ring, and guess what? That didn't work, either.

Next I stood up and paced from one end of my room

to the other. I do that sometimes when I'm trying to figure out stuff. We have this wood parquet floor and
counting the squares as I walk helps me concentrate.
It's twenty steps from one end of the room to the other,
if I don't skip any tiles. And after a few times across the
room, something occurred to me.

Not a suspect, though. Just a new place to look for
answers: Nancy Drew.

Obviously, Ivy had been teasing when she called
me Nancy Drew earlier. But she'd raised a good point.
Nancy was the most famous detective I'd ever heard of.
Yes, she's a fictional character, but it's not like I had
any real-life detectives to talk to.

Nancy Drew was the next best thing. And to her,
I had access.

That's how I found myself in the basement of our
building five minutes later, with the keys to our storage
locker in my hand.

The space is unfinished, which means the floors
are concrete and the walls are old splintered beams of
wood. A thick layer of dust coated everything in the
room, which was lit by a single bare bulb that hung
from a cord in the middle of the ceiling. Kind of spooky.
At least it would be if I were the type of person to get
nervous in these situations, but luckily I am not.

Our storage locker is in the back corner of the room.

When I opened the large metal door it creaked. I climbed over four bicycles, pushed past boxes of ski clothes, and scooted under my grandma's old dining room table (something my parents have held on to for when we move into a bigger place, which if you ask me will be never). And that's when I found my old box of books.

I opened it and pulled out the Nancy Drews from the bottom of the pile. My mom bought a dozen at a stoop sale a few years ago. Why? They were classics, she'd explained. Ones she'd adored as a child and assumed that I would, too. But here's my secret confession: I never made it beyond the beginning of book one. Nancy seemed too perfect. Her whole life was about helping people, which was nice and all, but not very realistic in my opinion. She didn't even go to school or have a job. And another thing? She and her friends never fought, and the entire town knew and adored her.

Nancy's whole world was one gigantic lovefest, but real life is messier. It's filled with clueless twin brothers and best friends who turn evil and mysterious dognappers and crushes who hardly know you exist and who won't even take out both earbuds to listen to what you have to say.

In short, I couldn't relate to Nancy or to her whole River Heights world. But I put all that aside because I wasn't looking for a great read. I was looking to solve a mystery. And Nancy seemed like a great place to start.

I didn't even head back upstairs. I just flopped down on one of Isabel's old velvet couches—ignoring the puff of dust that floated up—and cracked open book one, *The Secret of the Old Clock*.

The pages were yellow and brittle with age. They had to be turned carefully, and turn them I did. Pretty soon I couldn't stop. The story was much more exciting than I'd remembered—filled with snobby socialites, struggling heirs, an orphan, car chases, flat tires, widows, and false wills.

Nancy was as old-fashioned as I'd remembered, but she was way gutsy, too.

I got so into the story, I made it halfway through the book before I realized I was shivering. Not because I was scared or anything—just because it was drafty down in the basement, something that made no sense since it was warm outside. There wasn't a window in sight, so the underground room should've felt stuffy.

Yet I felt a breeze on the back of my neck. The door at the top of the stairs was still open, but if wind had blown in from there, I'd have felt it on my face.

I looked over my shoulder and noticed a quilt nailed to the wall behind me. Faded paisley patches of blue and burgundy rippled in the wind.

I walked closer and pulled it back, expecting to find a crack in the wall. Instead I found what looked like a handle. Then the whole blanket crumpled to the floor, revealing an entire door. Except it was tiny—no more than three feet high, like the entrance to a giant doll's house or maybe a troll's lair.

It reminded me of the crawl space in my bedroom. Each apartment had one, but they were no longer usable, just as Isabel had said—most emphatically—to Chloe the other day. Finn and I had tried to pry ours open a few times and the door never budged—at least not from the outside.

Of course, this door didn't look sealed shut at all. I slowly reached for the handle, but before I opened it I heard a scuffle.

And that's when I remembered Chloe's complaint: mice, which did freak me out. In a really big way.

I took a step back, right into a tall umbrella stand that crashed to the ground and made me scream.

"Hello?" The voice came from the top of the stairs.

"Isabel?" I called, hoping I'd heard my landlady's voice and not that of some giant talking rodent.

"Who's down there?" she asked.

"Just me." I picked up the quilt and reattached it to the wall.

"Maggie? What are you doing?"

"Nothing."

"Is everything okay?" she asked.

I grabbed a bunch of Nancy Drews, locked our storage locker, and made my way upstairs.

"I just had to get something from the basement," I said, showing Isabel the books.

She raised her reading glasses to her eyes and squinted at the title. "*The Secret of the Old Clock*. How wonderful!"

"You know it?" I asked.

"Know it?" replied Isabel. "They begged me to play Nancy Drew in one of the original movies."

"But you turned it down?"

"Of course!" said Isabel, looking surprised and pleased. "How did you know?"

I smiled. "Lucky guess."

Chapter 15

• • •

It's not like I ever expected Ivy to be my best friend again just because I was helping her find Kermit. I didn't want that. But I didn't think she'd ignore me, either. Yet that's exactly what happened at school on Monday. She didn't even say hi to me in English (the only class we share), and whenever we passed each other in the hall, she averted her gaze. Like I wasn't even there.

So I was completely surprised to find her sitting on my front stoop later that afternoon.

"What are you doing here?" I asked.

"We need to talk about Kermit." She said it like it was obvious.

"You couldn't have asked me at school?"

"That would've looked weird. I didn't want my friends asking a million questions. Plus, you didn't talk to me, either."

She had a point, actually. A few good ones, but I didn't say so. "Have you heard from the dognapper?"

"Nope. I was hoping you came up with something."

"Not yet." I shifted my bag from one shoulder to the other.

"It's weird being at home without him." Ivy rested her chin in her hands and stared off into space. "He used to sleep by my bed every night, then jump into it at, like, six thirty in the morning. I never even needed an alarm clock. Today I slept late and missed first period." She bit her bottom lip and glanced up at me for a quick second. "I could buy a clock, I guess, but that'd feel like giving up."

"It stinks. I know that," I said gently. "But don't give up. I'll find him."

Suddenly she glared at me and sat up straight. "You'd better find him, or else."

"Or else what?" I wondered what she could possibly threaten me with. She already acted like a total jerk most of the time *and* she'd ditched me for no good reason.

"Or else I'll tell Milo that you like him," she said, grinning mischievously.

"But that's—I don't like him." My voice came out squeaky with panic.

"You don't? Cool." She stood up and slipped on her sunglasses. "So that means you won't mind if I ask him out sometime. I mean, if you're not interested, I don't see any reason for me not to—"

"Wait, why would you? You don't even . . ."

Aargh! I couldn't believe she was pulling this.

"I thought you might need the extra motivation. You know, to find Kermit." She grabbed her book bag and took off down the street without another word.

"I'll find Kermit because he's a good dog," I called. "Not because of your threats."

Ivy didn't bother to reply. She didn't even turn around.

So I pulled out my keys and headed inside.

When I walked by the basement door, I noticed a giant padlock on it. Also, Glen was waiting outside Isabel's apartment. He was dressed in black cycling gear. His red and silver racing bike leaned against the wall. "Hey, Maggie. Is she home, do you know?"

"Isabel? She should be. Try knocking harder."

He pulled off his helmet and hung it on his handlebars. "I swear I heard her in there, but I've been knocking for five—"

Isabel opened the door before he finished his sentence.

"Maggie! I thought I heard your voice outside. You're just the girl I wanted to see."

"Do you still want me to take Preston to get his nails clipped?"

"Of course. Come in." Isabel opened the door wider to make room, and that's when she saw Glen standing next to me. "Oh, hello," she said, her voice shifting from warm to chilly in an instant.

"Isabel, do you have a moment?" asked Glen. "I was hoping to run something by you."

"I have many moments," said Isabel. "Why don't you come in for some tea and I'll tell you about the time I did summer stock with Mia Farrow?"

It was the kind of question that sounded more like an order. But Glen wasn't falling for it. "I'd like to replace one of the walls in my apartment," he said, ignoring Isabel's request.

"A wall?" Isabel seemed perplexed, and I didn't blame her.

"Yes, a wall in the studio." Glen leaned against the doorframe. "That back bedroom that I use as my studio, I mean. The sound quality is off and it's the strangest thing—every time I hit a low E note on my bass, the sound reverberates."

"Reverberates?" Isabel tilted her head to one side.

"Vibrates," Glen clarified.

"Yes, I know what reverberates means," she said. "I'm just trying to figure out why that would be."

"Me, too," said Glen. "It doesn't happen in any other room in the house. I noticed the problem ages ago, but I never gave it much thought. Not until the other day, when

I accidentally knocked over my bicycle. It hit the wall, which shook like it was made out of cardboard."

"It didn't break, did it?" asked Isabel.

"Nope," said Glen.

"No holes?"

"Not one."

"Did it scuff? Because when you move out you'll be responsible for any marks on the wall."

"It didn't scuff," said Glen, standing up straight. "And I'm not planning on moving out, unless you know something I don't."

"No." Isabel shook her head, frowning slightly. "Go on."

"So I checked out the wall and it seems kind of flimsy, which is weird because the rest of the walls in my place are so strong . . . almost like they're made out of a different material. So I was wondering, has anyone renovated? Maybe changed the structure of the place?"

"Well, I've only been here for twenty-five years," said Isabel. "I don't know what happened to the brownstone before I bought it, but there are certainly some quirks in the place. That's what happens in old buildings. And considering that this one was built by the legendary Al Flosso—"

"Who?" Glen asked.

"Al Flosso, the famous magician. I told you all about him when you moved in."

"You told me a famous *musician* lived here."

"Who knows?" Isabel shrugged. "Musicians probably lived here, too."

Glen shook his head, like he was trying to clear out some cobwebs. "Never mind. We're getting off track and I'm running late. So please just tell me, is it okay to fix it?"

Isabel frowned. "I don't think it's a good idea, starting up with construction."

"I'm willing to take care of the expense and all the work, too, if that's the issue. And it's just one wall."

"Which would change the integrity of the building," she said, sounding slightly British.

"I'm not sure that a building can have integrity, but please just think about it." As Glen backed away he waved to me. "See you later, Maggie."

"See you," I replied as he carried his bike upstairs.

"Reverberating walls." Isabel shook her head. "Have you ever heard such a thing?"

"Uh, no," I answered honestly, even though I suspected the question was rhetorical.

"Never be a landlady, Maggie. It's more trouble than it's worth. Now where was I? Oh yes. Mia Farrow."

"Actually, I'm here to pick up your dog for his nail appointment. Remember?" I leashed up Preston and headed for the door before Isabel could say much else.

The vet's office was on the corner of First Street

and Sixth Avenue in a space that used to be a restaurant. Some French place Ivy's parents took us to so we could celebrate her tenth birthday.

It was super fancy—crisp linen napkins, three kinds of bread in the basket, classical music playing softly in the background, and people speaking in voices no louder than whispers. Weird food on the menu— they actually served frogs' legs and snails and something called sweetbreads, which, according to Ivy's dad, is actually the pancreas of a baby cow. (Although I still wonder if he was messing with us.) In short, the meal was disgusting.

We were excited about dessert, though. We had spied the large cart in the corner stacked with shiny strawberry tarts, cloudlike fluffy meringues, and dark chocolate cakes speckled with flakes that looked like genuine gold. But when the waiter finally wheeled it over, Ivy accidentally sneezed on it. The waiter recoiled, looking down at us like we'd brought a family of cockroaches to dinner or worse, like we *were* a family of cockroaches. "I'll bring you your check now," he'd said, all snooty. And we burst out laughing. Then we headed to the Uncle Louie G ice-cream stand for root beer floats instead—a delicious ending to a horrible meal.

The restaurant disappeared a while ago and no one missed it. The space had been vacant for over a year. Now the sign read DR. REESE, LICENSED VETERINARIAN out front. Inside, a row of chairs lined the lobby area and a receptionist sat at a large desk behind a small silver computer.

Framed paintings of fluffy puppies and cuddly looking kittens lined the walls.

"I'll be with you in a moment," the woman said. Her red hair was slicked back into a ponytail and she wore large glasses. She looked familiar, but this didn't exactly shock me. Park Slope is such a small neighborhood, I always see familiar faces.

"Take your time," I said, following Preston, who needed to sniff something in the corner.

The woman typed for a few moments longer and then looked up and smiled. "This must be Preston."

"How did you know?" I asked.

"It's been a slow morning. Slow summer, honestly. But I just opened two months ago, so I'm hoping things will pick up."

"Oh."

"I'm Dr. Reese."

Last time I took Preston to the vet, all the doctors were in the back and three receptionists handled the patients. I tried to hide my surprise as we shook hands, but Dr. Reese seemed to pick up on my train of thought.

"The receptionist just quit," she said immediately. "You must've made your appointment with Blaire. She only lasted two weeks because she was allergic to animals. Can you imagine taking a job at a vet's office with that kind of condition? She said she hadn't thought it would be a problem. I told her that was the dumbest thing I'd ever heard, and then she quit on the spot. I've got the worst luck!" Dr. Reese smiled at me. "Your dog is beautiful. He's an Irish wolfhound, right?"

"He is. And actually, he belongs to my neighbor, Isabel Rose Franini? She's the one who made the appointment."

"Oh yes, I remember," said Dr. Reese. "She's the Broadway star."

"You've heard of her?" I asked.

"No, but she made sure to tell me who she was. Shall we?" The doctor gestured toward two swinging doors, which led to a row of exam rooms. Preston and I followed her into the first one. It had a small platform at the center, two chairs on the side, and a bunch of animal anatomy posters on the walls. Skeletal views of a cat, dog, lizard, rabbit, and bird.

The whole place smelled strongly of disinfectant. In the background I heard dogs whimpering—something that made Preston nervous. His whole body shook as he pulled toward the door. Like he'd finally figured out where he was and what went on there.

"Nervous dog, huh?" asked Dr. Reese.

"Aren't they all?" I asked.

"Some more than others."

Suddenly a ferocious growl came from the back of the building. Then I heard a scuffle that sounded like a dogfight.

Dr. Reese glanced at the door. "Be right back."

When she returned a few moments later, I asked, "Other patients acting up?"

"Yes, it's a zoo back there." She laughed to herself. "Well, not exactly, but you know what I mean." Dr. Reese patted the platform with one hand. "He needs to be up here."

Preston didn't want to get up on the table, and once we convinced him to, he tucked his tail between his legs and started trembling again.

"It's okay, Preston. This isn't going to hurt at all," said Dr. Reese.

She spoke to Preston in a calm and soothing voice. Then she stroked his front legs, softly and steadily. Moments later, when she lifted up one of his paws, Preston hardly noticed. Clearly Dr. Reese knew what she was doing.

"This will be over before you know it," she promised as she picked up the nail clippers with her free hand.

Clip, clip, clip—the scissors flew and she moved onto Preston's next paw without incident.

As I watched Dr. Reese work, I realized she looked really familiar. Not like I'd simply passed her on the street, but like I knew her. I just couldn't quite place her. Not until I glanced down and saw that she had on black high heels. I'd heard them clicking against the tile floor when she walked and I didn't know why I hadn't realized it before . . .

"You're Brenda, right?" I asked. "Of Boutique Breeds by Brenda."

Dr. Reese's whole body seemed to stiffen. She looked up at me, alarmed. And once she met my gaze, I was sure of it.

"I ran into you last week, outside the Pizza Den. You had a dog in your purse and—"

"I'd never carry a dog in my purse," Dr. Reese said as she moved on to Preston's back paws. "And I've no idea what you're talking about."

She seemed unhappy—like I'd said something offensive, so I backpedaled. "I'm sorry, but I ran into someone with a stack of flyers. She looked just like you. And I didn't actually see the dog. I just heard it."

"Nope. Wasn't me." Something about the way she stared me down made me doubt myself.

"Um, okay. I guess I was wrong."

Dr. Reese sighed and put down the nail clippers. She'd already finished—that's how good she was. Not just gentle but stealthy. I was impressed. "My twin sister is named Brenda. Maybe it's her you ran into? She's got a dog-breeding business in the neighborhood."

"You're a twin?" I asked.

She nodded. "Some people think we look alike, but I don't see it. I'm sorry. I guess I'm a bit sensitive."

I knew how she felt. No one mixes me up with Finn anymore, but sometimes people make weird assumptions. Like since he's a good soccer player, some people assume that I must be a big jock, too. Or sometimes it's the opposite. Because I do well in school, they think Finn must do poorly, like we can't both have the same talents because we once shared a womb. It's dumb. Anyway, I was about to tell her that I had a twin brother, but before I had the chance, Preston leaped off the table and bolted for the door. He stared up at the doorknob and whimpered, desperate to get out.

"Not time to go yet, buddy," said Dr. Reese. "We still need to do your exam."

"Oh, we're just here for his nails," I said.

Dr. Reese smiled brightly. "Free exam with every nail clipping. This week's special." She knelt down, raised her stethoscope to her ears, and placed the round end to Preston's chest before I could protest. Not that I would've—Isabel would be psyched about the free checkup.

At least that's what I thought until I noticed the troubled expression on Dr. Reese's face.

"Something wrong?" I asked.

Rather than answer me, Dr. Reese turned to her laptop and began typing. "I just need to look something up. I'm sure it's nothing, but—" Suddenly she gasped and raised her hand to her chest. "Oh dear."

"What is it?"

"I'm afraid his heart is racing at an alarming speed, which is symptomatic of a very rare heart condition. How old is Preston?"

"He's just four," I said.

"Four. How interesting." Dr. Reese's voice seemed flat, almost like she was disappointed. Then she stared at him some more. "He does look younger, though. Could almost pass for a puppy. Does he have any other health problems?"

"No, not that I know of."

"I'm glad to hear that," Dr. Reese said, frowning at him. "But I'm concerned with the way he's panting."

We both studied Preston, who stared right back at us, pink tongue out, chest heaving. True, he panted pretty hard. But it was warm in Dr. Reese's office. Plus, new places made him nervous. And didn't all dogs pant?

"I thought that's how dogs cool off," I said, suddenly remembering something I'd read in a book on dog care. "It's what they do since they can't sweat, right?"

Dr. Reese chuckled, like she'd just heard

something crazy. "Oh, Maggie. I understand why you want everything to be okay with Preston, but I'm going to need to talk to your parents about him."

"He's not my dog, remember? He belongs to my neighbor, Isabel. She's the one who made the appointment."

"Oh yes. Please have Ms. Franini call me as soon as possible. I'm afraid he's going to need surgery, and soon."

"I don't understand this," I said as she rushed us out the door. "Preston seems so healthy."

"That's the problem with the heart," said Dr. Reese. "You never know when it's really sick."

Chapter 16

• • •

"You'll be fine," I told Preston as we headed out of Dr. Reese's office. "Whatever the problem is, we'll get it taken care of." His eyes seemed bright and there was a spring in his step. So excited to be out of the vet's office, he didn't notice the nervous tremor in my voice.

But rather than reassure me, his good mood made me feel worse. Poor guy had no idea of the trouble that lay ahead. I decided to stop at Beastly Bites and buy him a rawhide chew. It's the dog equivalent of buying ice cream with rainbow sprinkles to make you feel better after a lousy day.

Not that Preston knew he had anything to feel bad about. I'm the one who needed the chew. Er, ice cream. Because Preston's happy innocence made me cringe with dread.

Before I got to the pet store, I noticed an elderly

woman stop in front of the Key Food and tie her golden retriever to a parking meter. She bent down to whisper something to the dog, then patted him on the head and went into the store. She dragged her folded-up red shopping cart behind her.

Lucy and I developed this theory a while back that everyone in our neighborhood sports some kind of wheels, and what you have depends on your age. Babies are in strollers and toddlers on tricycles or in wagons. When you turn five or thereabouts, you graduate to Razor scooters and bikes and maybe some in-line skates, just for the sake of variety. Then at seventeen, real scooters and cars. Which you keep for years and years. Finally, when you get really old, you wheel around one of those fold-up shopping carts. Or you're back to getting wheeled around again, but this time in a wheelchair. It all comes full circle.

Anyway, this lady had silver hair and a shopping cart, which meant she was most likely someone's grandma—quite possibly someone's great grandma.

Her dog was adorable, but seeing him tied up like that—alone on the sidewalk—made me feel sick inside because it reminded me of poor Kermit.

I'd been so preoccupied worrying about Preston, I'd almost forgotten about Ivy's dog. And Ivy's threats.

But now the awful memories came back in a rush: how Kermit was gone and I'd messed up his safe return.

I wished I could go back in time to Saturday.

If I hadn't walked in on Ivy trying to steal from me, I never would've gotten involved. Which meant Kermit would be safe at home. And I wouldn't have to deal with Ivy's dumb threats about Milo.

But it was too late for that.

I kept my eyes peeled in case I spotted Jane or someone else with a Dial-A-Walker sweatshirt. Parminder and Cassie hadn't yet called me back. And their silence made me nervous.

The old woman's golden retriever was on the yellow side of gold, and fluffy like a baby lion cub. He stretched out on the sidewalk, resting his big head between furry paws. He seemed content, happy to wait and happy to be out on this beautiful early fall day. Most people who passed by didn't even notice him. But a few waved and one guy even reached down to give him a scratch behind his ears.

The dog lifted his head and smiled, if dogs can smile, and wagged his tail like he was the luckiest animal around.

It warmed my heart. At least for the moment. Then everything changed quite suddenly.

The guy stood up and taped something familiar-looking to the parking meter: a blue index card.

My gut felt queasy, filled with dread. I couldn't believe it—I didn't want to.

But a moment later, the guy untied the dog and led him away.

Just took him.

I blinked.

Then I blinked again.

My heart pounded so hard, I feared it would bust out of my chest and bounce down the street.

I gripped Preston's leash tighter, hardly believing I'd just witnessed a dognapping.

Yet it happened right in front of me. I hadn't even seen the guy's face!

The dognapper was here. And he was getting away.

I opened my mouth to scream but no sound came out. I guess I was in shock because I couldn't move, either. I had to follow him—I knew I did—but my legs stuck to the sidewalk like my boot soles were caked in superglue.

I should've yelled. I needed to chase him.

Tackle him.

Get up in his face and scream, "How could you?"

Or, "What's wrong with you?"

Or more to the point, "Where's Kermit?"

But as quickly as he'd appeared and stolen the dog, he was gone.

He'd turned the corner swiftly and headed down

Garfield. The dog followed happily—tail swishing through the air, with no idea of how wrong this was.

I focused on moving, commanded my body to act, and managed to take one step. Then another, and another, until I got to the end of the street.

Preston was game—up for the chase—although he's always up for anything.

We turned the corner. With clenched fists and an aching heart, I couldn't figure out what to do first. Grab him? Or scream, "Thief!"

If I screamed he might run.

Tackling him would catch him off guard. And I was pretty sure I could bring him down.

I knew kung fu!

Okay, fine, I'd only been taking classes for a few months. I'm just a level one white belt. But still . . . I'm not the worst kid in the class.

This guy seemed taller than me, but not by much. Way skinnier, too.

Crazy, since all this time I'd assumed Kermit's dog-napper was some sinister adult—Jane or some big intimidating guy with a grubby goatee and long bushy sideburns. Maybe a tattoo of a pitchfork on his neck. Nancy Drew's villains were always so, well, villainous.

But this guy was no thug—he was just a kid. And from the looks of it, he seemed close to my age.

He had long, dark floppy hair and was dressed in faded jeans and a navy blue sweater. As I got closer I noticed that the sweater had a big hole in one shoulder and—wait a second.

I stopped suddenly, catching Preston by surprise. He looked up at me as if to ask, "Huh?"

My voice came out in a whisper. "Sorry, guy."

He tried tugging me forward but I could not take another step.

It was the sweater that stopped me.

The lack of a sweater, to be more accurate. I knew that hole. Just like I knew that boy.

The dognapper, that is.

He was Milo.

Chapter 17

• • •

Milo. Yeah, *that* Milo.

Somehow, someway, in some crazy universe, I had spied the dognapper in action.

But spying on the dognapper wasn't the worst part.

I had fallen for a dognapper.

I'd lain awake thinking about him.

Lost sleep over him.

Wasted precious time daydreaming about him.

But how was it possible that cute and thoughtful, seemingly sweet, chess-playing and expert-leaning Milo stole dogs?

Why would he possibly do this? It made no sense. And yet, it explained so much. Or at least why he'd acted so weird in the park last week. His odd behavior had nothing to do with me. He couldn't take the time to tell me the name of his precious dog because it wasn't his dog. That poor fluffy creature was just another victim. He probably hadn't even known her name. But wait a second . . .

He had to have known her name because that was a part of his dognapping scam.

If Ivy's experience taught me anything it was this: Milo prepared ransom notes in advance.

Which meant that he was more devious than I'd thought.

My mind raced to make sense of his evil scheming, and then it hit me. How he made it work.

Milo must choose his dogs ahead of time. Prepare notes and have them at the ready. That meant he'd followed this poor grandma. Waited for her to leave her golden retriever alone so he could kidnap the poor guy and hold him for ransom.

A premeditated crime.

But why? For the money?

If Jane were guilty, at least she would've had a bit more motivation. Revenge is one thing. But stealing dogs for cold hard cash? Heartless!

I was stunned. Sick to my stomach. Absolutely horrified.

Crushed by my crush, and in the most unimaginable way possible.

But I had to do something. If only I could think straight.

I shook my head to focus. The sidewalks were

crowded with people. Some rushed to the subway. Others meandered by with yoga mats slung across their backs. The chubby, sweating mail carrier huffed as he wheeled his mail cart up the street. A high school–age hipster slouched by in skinny jeans that showed too much boxer. Of course, any boxer is too much boxer in my opinion. Underwear is called underwear for a reason.

But Milo? He was nowhere to be seen. He'd disappeared in the crowd. I had to find him.

I walked down Seventh Avenue, past First Street. It seemed as if only a moment had passed when I found myself on Eleventh. I marched past kids having races on their scooters and a couple of girls taking turns bouncing on a pogo stick. Three ice-cream shops and four frozen-yogurt stores. Five places claiming to serve the best pizza. Two stoop sales and four baby boutiques. No, five. Make that six.

Over an hour passed and I never found Milo or the poor golden retriever.

And then I realized my other mistake. Instead of following Milo, I should've returned to the scene of the crime so I could tell that unlucky woman that I knew what happened to her dog.

I hurried back to the Key Food. But of course, I was too late. The grandma was gone and so was the note.

Another dog stolen, held for ransom. This time I'd come close to saving him, but I had failed miserably. And now there was nothing I could do about it.

Or was there?

I hurried to the nearest pay phone, intent on calling the police, but then I realized that Ivy had already done that and it hadn't worked.

So I turned around and hurried Preston home.

I still had to tell Isabel about her poor dog's heart condition.

Not to mention walk Bean and Milo.

Aargh!

When I finally gave Isabel the bad news, I almost broke down in tears.

"But I don't understand," said Isabel, dropping to her knees and hugging her dog. "He seems so healthy. This has got to be some sort of mistake."

"You think?"

"Yes, it must be. Let's not jump to any conclusions, anyway. I'll get a second opinion and everything will be just fine."

"But what if he needs surgery? There could be complications." I was thinking of Beckett, the toddler I'd run into last week. The one whose dog, Cookie, went in for surgery and ended up "on the farm." I didn't want the same thing to happen to Preston. I couldn't imagine it. I almost wished I were still young enough to believe in some faraway farm as the final destination of all lost pets.

Isabel gave me a hug. "Please don't worry. It's too soon to get this worked up. I promise you, we'll get to the bottom of this."

I hoped she was right.

As soon as I got outside, I ran down the street and let myself into Cassie's apartment so I could collect Bean. I didn't bother putting on her sweater because there wasn't enough time. I just leashed her up and headed out. And it may have been my imagination, but she seemed happier without the weight of the clothes. Meaning, she snarled at only one other dog during our whole twenty-minute walk. When we got back to her house, I scrawled a quick note to Cassie:

Doggie Deets

FROM THE DESK OF
MAGGIE BROOKLYN

No need to get Bean's purple dress dry-cleaned because she didn't actually wear it.

Then I headed upstairs. When I let myself into Parminder's apartment, I was surprised to find her there.

"Maggie, is that you?" she called as she headed around the corner.

"Yeah, sorry I'm late! I had to bring another dog to the vet, and it took a lot longer than I'd thought, and, well . . ." Not knowing what to say next, I stumbled over my words. It had been a strange day and I still felt weird seeing Parminder in her living room, outside of school. Calling her Parminder instead of Ms. Patel made me feel grown-up. Maybe too much so, considering everything going on.

"Oh, don't worry about it. Milo is fine."

Yeah, dog-Milo is perfect, I thought. It's boy-Milo who's a total psycho.

"And I'm sorry I didn't call you back yesterday," said Parminder. "You said you had a question about Milo's old walker? Is everything okay?"

"Her name is Jane, right?"

"Yes." Parminder nodded. "Jane from Dial-A-Walker. She walked him for about a year."

"I ran into her last week. She recognized Bean, and I happened to mention Milo and—"

"And she was upset, wasn't she?" asked Parminder.

"A little," I admitted. "So what happened?" It didn't matter anymore. I knew Jane was innocent, but I was still curious.

"It's quite simple," said Parminder. "Her company raised their fees by fifteen percent and it got too expensive."

"So you fired her because of a fee increase?"

"Yes," said Parminder. "Although firing sounds so harsh. I prefer to think of it as not being able to afford her services anymore. I told her it was nothing personal."

"And how did she take the news?"

Parminder cringed. "Well, she wasn't pleased, but she wasn't willing to compromise, either. She said it was company policy. I reminded her that she owned the company, which meant it was all up to her, but apparently that didn't matter."

"Does she have employees? Other walkers, I mean?"

"I don't know." Parminder shrugged. "I always assumed so, but I've only ever dealt with Jane."

This seemed weird, but I didn't say so. I just leashed up Milo and took him for an extra long walk, since I'd kept him waiting.

And also? I needed to think.

I had so many questions.

Why did Milo steal dogs? Where did he keep them? And what was he planning on doing with them all? How was I going to get Kermit back safely? And what about that grandma's golden retriever and Lassie, the missing collie on the sign?

Should I confront Milo? Demand that he return all the dogs at once?

He'd just deny it.

But I'd seen him with my very own eyes . . .

I got so caught up in thought, I didn't even pay attention to where I was until a booming clap of thunder echoed through the sky. Next came a bright flash of lightning that violently interrupted the dusk. Dog-Milo and I were already on Fifteenth Street. Far from home—both his and mine.

I turned around and headed back as quickly as I could. The next crack of thunder made me jump. Dog-Milo whimpered and I didn't blame him.

One second the skies were sunny, and now suddenly all was grim. First came a steady drizzle. Then the skies just opened up. Rain poured down as if from a high-powered faucet. I was drenched before I even made it into the deli.

"No dogs allowed!" barked the owner from behind the counter.

"I'll just be a second," I said. "All I need is an umbrella." I picked one up and put it on the counter. Reached into my backpack and pulled out my wallet. Opened it up and saw I only had two dollars. I gulped. "Um, how much is that?"

"Six dollars," said the owner.

"Do you have anything cheaper?" I asked.

"There's one for five dollars in the back of the store, but you can't bring the dog."

"Do you have any for two dollars?" I asked, holding up all the money I had.

He shook his head and asked, "Are you kidding?"

Even if I had been, I doubt he'd have laughed.

I bought a newspaper instead. Tented it over my head and jogged toward Parminder's.

And just when I thought I couldn't get wetter, just when I thought I was soaked to the bone, it started raining harder. The newspaper dripped, then split in two. I threw out the wetter half and tried holding the other one over my head, but it quickly turned to soggy confetti. And I still had eight blocks to go. I threw out the paper scraps and kept running.

Moving so fast I ran right into someone.

"Sorry," I said.

"Maggie?" asked a familiar—and very surprised—voice.

Looking up, I found myself face-to-face with my dad.

"Hi!" I said. "Um, got a spare umbrella?"

He shifted his over to shelter me from the rain. "You look like a wet rat."

"Thanks, Dad. What are you doing in Brooklyn?"

"I'm working here."

"Really? In the neighborhood?" I couldn't believe this.

"The piece I'm shooting is on the Brooklyn Dodgers, Maggie. Think about it."

In response to my blank stare he added, "That means I'm filming in Brooklyn."

"Oh." I gulped. "Right."

I glanced at dog-Milo, then tried to step in front of him, but it was too late.

"And who's this?" asked Dad, gesturing toward my favorite puggle, now drenched and unhappily so.

"This is Milo." I cringed, hoping the inquiry would end there. "And I should really get him out of the rain. Okay? I'll just drop him off and come right home."

"Uh, Maggie?" asked Dad. "Whose dog is that?"

"Parminder's." I said it like it was obvious. As if I'd already told him six times. "Ms. Patel, I mean. She was my third grade teacher, remember? Finn's, too."

"Yes, I remember Ms. Patel." He looked from me to Milo. "I just don't understand why you're walking her dog."

I smiled. Shrugged. Tried to keep my face from turning red. "He needed to go out?"

"*Maggie?*" Dad didn't sound happy.

I sighed. "It's kind of a long story."

Chapter 18

. . .

"A dog walker?" Dad said, like he'd never heard of such a thing.

"How long has this been going on?" asked Mom. Her voice sounded surprised, horrified, and angry all at the same time—a tone that hinted at a harsh punishment if I didn't play my cards right. Not that I had any cards left. Not even ones that didn't count, like the joker or the too-tiny printed instructions.

By the time I'd gotten home and changed into dry clothes, my mom was back from work and my dad had filled her in.

Now the three of us sat in the living room. Me on one side, them—arms crossed and faces crosser—on the other.

They needed some sort of explanation, but I couldn't figure out which parts of the truth were safe to tell.

Meanwhile, the smells of dinner—chicken and vegetable teriyaki stir-fry—wafted in from the nearby kitchen and made my stomach growl. Torture!

"Maybe we can talk about this over dinner?" I suggested.

"There'll be no eating until you explain yourself," said Mom, who really knew how to turn on the pressure.

"I've only been doing it for a few weeks." I pulled a throw pillow onto my lap and tugged at a loose thread. "And it's only a few dogs."

"I can't believe you started a business without telling us," said Dad.

"It was an accident."

"You accidentally started a business?" asked Mom. "I don't really see how that's possible."

I shrugged. There were so many more important things to deal with. Kermit. The golden retriever. Ivy and her stupid threats about Milo. Milo himself. Not to mention Preston and his potential surgery.

This was the worst, most inconvenient time to get caught.

"Can you try to explain?" asked Dad.

"And stop pulling at that thread," said Mom.

I pushed the pillow aside and squirmed in my seat, not knowing where to begin.

"Well, I only walk three dogs."

"And when, with all this dog walking, are you going to find the time to do your homework?" Mom asked.

"It hasn't been a problem yet."

"'Yet' is the key word," Dad said. "School's only just started. It's going to get harder."

"And what about oil painting and kung fu?" asked Mom.

"I don't walk dogs other than Preston over the weekend, and this is exactly why I couldn't tell you in the first place."

"So you lied?" asked Mom in full trial-attorney mode. "You're not exactly making the most valid case here."

I swallowed hard and tried to explain. "I didn't lie. It just never came up and you guys knew I walked Preston. So I figured, what's two more dogs?"

"It could be dangerous, going into strangers' apartments," Mom said.

"I agree, and that's why none of my clients is a stranger. Parminder I know, and Cassie is her neighbor. And it's not like I'm looking for other clients. Three dogs is my limit. Two that I'm getting paid for and Preston. And walking *him* was your idea. Plus, none of it takes up very much time. Two hours tops. I'm always home by five."

"You mean you're always home before us," Dad pointed out. "So you don't get caught."

"Well, that kinda backfired tonight," I said.

"It's the sneaking around that concerns me," Mom said. "The lying and—"

"I never lied."

"You started a business behind our backs," Dad said.

"You never *asked* me if I was a dog walker. If you had, I'd have told you. Anyway, you let me babysit, which is even more time-consuming. And this is kind of the same thing . . ."

"Except we only let you babysit on weekends," Mom pointed out. "Having a job every single day after school? That's too much. You need time to focus on your studies. Seventh grade is important. You'll be in high school soon and—"

"In two more years!" I said. "That's forever away. Please don't make me quit. If you do I'll be leaving lots of people in the lurch. Not to mention being forced to destroy a very lucrative career."

"It's hardly a career," Mom said.

"For some people it is," I replied, thinking of crabby Jane. Not that I wanted to be anything like her. Even though I did feel kind of bad now for thinking she was the dognapper.

"That's true," Dad admitted. "You know, I used to walk dogs when I was in film school. It was a fun gig."

"Really?" I asked. "How come you never told me?"

He shrugged. "It never came up."

"Did it get in the way of your studies?"

My father didn't answer. So I knew I'd made my point. Now I had to kick up the pleading. "Please don't ground me. I'm sorry I didn't tell you and I know it was wrong to deceive you. Honestly, I never meant to. And I won't let it interfere with my studies. Who knows? It might even look good for college because, you know, it shows that I can be resourceful. Responsible, too. Hardworking. Trustworthy."

"You do make some good points," Mom admitted. "And if you'd come to us ahead of time, it would be a different story."

"Yeah, a very short story because you guys would've said no."

My parents looked at each other. But not like they were mad at me. More like they were trying to figure out what to do, which gave me hope. A little, anyway.

"Want me to set the table?" I asked.

"Finn already did," Mom said. "He's been home all afternoon."

Of course he had.

"Look, your father and I will discuss this later. Go get your brother. Tell him dinner will be ready in five."

I stood up, headed for the back of the apartment, then turned around. "I really am sorry. I should've told you. You're right. But please don't make me give it up."

"We'll talk later," Dad said.

And he couldn't have sounded more ominous if he'd tried.

Chapter 19

. . .

When I got to our room I found Finn playing Super Mario Brothers on his Wii. Technically the Wii belongs to both of us, but I hadn't played since the week after we got it.

"Yo," he said. "Guess what?"

"Not in the mood." I walked right past him, threw myself facedown on my bed, and rested my head in my arms. I did not move.

"You okay?" asked Finn.

I sighed, almost too upset to explain. "Mom and Dad found out about the dog walking."

"Yeah, they asked me if I knew anything about it," said Finn.

I propped myself up on my elbows. "And?"

"And I said no, but that it sounds like a cool idea."

"You said that?" I asked.

Finn shrugged. "Sure."

"Thanks."

"No biggie," said Finn. "And you're really going to thank me in a minute."

I'd no idea what he was talking about, but at the moment I didn't care. I flipped over onto my back and rubbed my eyes. This was impossible. I had to do something. Had to talk to Milo—to tell him to return Kermit. But what if he got angry? What if he refused? What if he threatened me?

If the guy steals innocent animals, who knows what else he's capable of? Clearly I didn't know him at all.

"Tell me I'm the best brother in the entire world," said Finn.

"Huh?" I looked over at him, confused.

He stood at the foot of my bed, a proud smile on his face. I figured he was going to tell me he'd gotten to the sixth-level galaxy in Super Mario. Although that wouldn't make him the best brother in the world—only the best gamer in the house, which he already was, but only for a lack of any real competition.

"I know you've been mad since our party," he went on. "And I'm sorry about inviting Ivy and Company. It wasn't fair. I've been feeling bad about it ever since."

Finn never admitted when he was wrong. Maybe I'd been too quick to call him clueless.

"It's fine," I said.

"No, I saw how you two came out of our room that night. After I asked you to get poker chips? Not talking. How your face was pale. And how you never actually got the chips. And I know Ivy turned kind of evil. I just never thought she'd act that way at our party."

"Don't worry about it," I said. And I meant it. I didn't need to hold a grudge against Finn.

"Well, I've already made it up to you."

"And how'd you do that?" I would've asked anyway, just to humor him. But the truth was, I could use the distraction. Anything to take my mind off Milo and what I had to do.

"Remember Amber?" he asked.

"Are you guys back together?" I wondered.

"Nope," said Finn. "She won't even speak to me. What I mean is, remember the 'bait and switch'?"

"Yeah, of course." Last spring, when Finn had a crush on Amber Greyson, I invited her to the movies and then faked a fever at the last minute. We were supposed to meet at the Pavilion—that's the closest multiplex— but Finn went instead, with my apologies and his offer to accompany her in my place. She was so charmed, the two of them ended up going out for six whole weeks.

He never even told her that my fever was phony. To this day she still probably thought her first date with Finn was a lucky accident.

Or maybe now she thought of it as unlucky,

considering that Finn broke up with her two weeks before school got out.

He did it once he found out she'd be at sleepaway camp in Maine for two months. Amber promised to write to him every week. And Finn panicked, realizing that *he*'d be expected to write letters back. It all sounded like too much work, so he told her long-distance relationships were complicated. She was stunned and wanted more of an explanation. But Finn couldn't tell her the whole truth because even he realized that his actual reason made him look lazy and kind of callous, too.

"*Do* you want to get back together with her?" I asked. "Because I don't think that's going to work. She's still pretty bent out of shape over being dumped on her birthday."

"It was the day before her birthday," Finn said. "That's when I tried IMing her, anyway. It's not my fault she didn't get the message right away."

"Oh right." I laughed. "Um, somehow I don't think that was the problem, exactly."

"This has nothing to do with Amber," Finn insisted. "I'm talking about the bait and switch. One of the best things you've ever come up with. And I think it's time I returned the favor."

"But I don't like anyone."

"Come on." Finn rolled his eyes. "You think I don't know about your crush on Milo Sanchez?"

"Don't say his name."

"What's the big deal?"

"I don't like him."

"What am I, completely clueless?" asked Finn.

"You really want me to answer that?"

"Definitely not."

Suddenly I saw where he was going with this. And I couldn't let it happen. I sat up. "Finn, I'm serious. I do not like Milo! It's very nice of you to want to help me out, but please don't. There's a lot going on in my life. Stuff you don't know about. Stuff you don't *want* to know about."

"Why all the crazy talk?" he asked, kicking back on his bed and tossing his Nerf mini football into the air. "I'm only trying to help."

"Okay, fine. I'll admit that I *used* to like Milo."

Finn raised his left eyebrow, a move he perfected last summer. "Used to as in last week?"

Used to as in two hours ago, I thought but didn't say. "It's complicated. But trust me, he's not who I thought he was. So promise me you're not going to make plans with him."

"Too late," said Finn. "He's coming over tomorrow afternoon."

"No!"

"I knew if I asked ahead of time you'd say no, and I didn't want you to chicken out. We're supposed to play soccer in the park. Or Pro Evolution Soccer on the Wii if it rains. Turns out he's got the latest version, which has been back-ordered at GameStop for ages." Finn felt his forehead. "But I've definitely been feeling sick."

This was insane. I flopped back down on my bed and thought about yesterday's scene in the park. Ivy breaking up the soccer game. All those angry guys. Clearly a bad omen.

"I hate soccer."

This wasn't technically true, but it was all I could think to say.

"You don't have to play soccer with him," Finn said. "You two should grab a slice at the Pizza Den. No, not the Pizza Den. Go somewhere datelike. Two Boots, maybe? Or the Cocoa Bar for hot chocolate and giant marshmallows? Maybe see a movie?"

I groaned. And not just because I had to get dating advice from my brother, which would've been bad enough.

"Don't thank me or anything." Finn seemed so pleased, like he'd done something brilliant.

I pulled my pillow over my face and screamed.

Kermit was missing.

My parents were on the verge of grounding me.

Preston might need major surgery.

And now I had a date with the dognapper.

Chapter 20

◆ ◆ ◆

My parents didn't ground me but, for once, I wished they had. If they'd grounded me I would've had the perfect excuse not to hang out with Milo on Tuesday. But no. They actually took what I said seriously and acted in a reasonable manner. The one time I wanted them to freak out and overreact!

On a brighter note, they weren't going to make me stop walking dogs. I just had to promise never to lie to them again.

And to be home by six o'clock every night.

And not to take on any more clients without asking them first.

And to keep up my grades, which wouldn't be a problem. I'd have plenty of time for studying once I managed to rescue Kermit and the other missing dogs. But for now, it was all I could think about.

I spent my lunch period in the library, avoiding Ivy

and Milo and finishing another Nancy Drew novel—
The Hidden Staircase—but it didn't give me any new
ideas. In fact, of the entire dozen books in my collection,
Nancy didn't have to deal with one kidnapped dog.
Clearly I had to find my answers elsewhere.

As soon as school got out I took Preston to the park.
He wanted to play fetch with this yellow Lab named
Sprout, but I didn't want him to overdo it, what with his
possible heart condition, so we just walked around.

After dropping him off I collected Bean, who snarled
at the mail carrier almost as soon as we got to the sidewalk. We just circled the block.

When I walked dog-Milo down Third Street, I saw a
familiar blond toddler drawing rainbows on the sidewalk. His mom sat on the stoop in the shade, reading
The New Yorker.

"Hey, Beckett," I said.

Looking up, he narrowed his eyes at me in suspicion. He seemed to be asking, "Do I know you?" with
his silent glare.

"We met when I was walking Bean," I said. "The
little Maltese who looks like—"

"Cookie!" Beckett yelled. He stood up and placed
his chubby hands on his tiny hips.

"Yes, Cookie."

His mom smiled at me. "You have two dogs?" she
asked.

"Actually, I have none. I'm just a dog walker."

"Oh, I didn't realize. I should get your number."

"You have a new dog?" I asked.

"We're planning on getting another one," she replied. "But I think I'll do a little more research this time. Get one with a better temperament."

"Good idea," I said, thinking if Cookie were anything like Bean personality-wise, well, that would be something to avoid.

Not that it made her story any less tragic . . .

Of course, thinking of Cookie's fate made me scared for Preston all over again.

"Can I ask you something?" I said to her, staring down at Beckett and trying to figure out how to put it delicately. "Um, I was wondering about the circumstances of Cookie's . . . trip to the farm."

He rolled his eyes and dropped to the sidewalk once more. This time he drew a truck with red chalk. Then shaded it purple.

His mom set her magazine aside, stood up, and walked over. "She had to have heart surgery," she whispered as she bent down to pet Milo. "And there were complications."

"I'm so sorry. Maybe I shouldn't have brought it up."

"No, it's okay. The poor dog had a very rare heart defect and the doctor warned us that the surgery was risky. But doing nothing would have been even more dangerous . . . That's what we were told, anyway. And, well, you know the rest."

As I listened to her story I got the shivers. Because it wasn't just sad—it sounded eerily familiar. "Who was Cookie's doctor?"

"She's right in the neighborhood, unfortunately, which means I can't walk down Sixth Avenue without getting teary-eyed." Beckett's mom's eyes welled up now, even just talking about poor Cookie.

"Sixth Avenue? Are you talking about Dr. Reese?"

Beckett's mom seemed surprised. "You know her?"

"I just took a client there yesterday. When did this all happen?"

"About a month ago." She shrugged. "Maybe longer. Why do you ask?"

"Just wondering," I said, backing away. "Thanks for letting me know, and good luck with the new dog."

"Wait, do you have a card?" she asked.

"A card?"

"For your dog-walking business."

"Oh right. I don't have one yet. But here . . ." I pulled a piece of Doggie Deets stationery from my bag, wrote down my number, and handed it over.

"Maggie," Beckett's mom read. "Nice to meet you, Maggie. I'm Lisa and you know Beckett, of course."

"Of course," I repeated.

"I'll call you as soon as we get that new dog."

"Okay, thanks," I replied as I waved good-bye. "And see you later, Beckett."

Beckett looked up and frowned at me. "Tell Cookie I say hi," he said.

"Honey, Cookie is at the farm and Maggie has never even met her," his mom assured him.

Same drill, different day, but I didn't stick around to hear it.

I hurried dog-Milo home so I could prepare for my date with boy-Milo, who, I suppose, should really be referred to as jerk-Milo.

Chapter 21

◆ ◆ ◆

Ten minutes later I stared into my half of the closet, with no idea what to wear.

My favorite jeans smelled like dogs and my backup jeans had just come out of the wash, so they felt way too stiff. Wearing a skirt would be trying too hard, and I had the same problem with leggings. Luckily my navy blue cords were clean and perfectly broken in. Now I only had to worry about a top. I looked too much like an American flag in my red-and-white-striped waffle tee. So I put on a plain lavender shirt instead. "Plain" was the key word. Milo was no one I should be trying to impress. In fact, he could be dangerous. That's why I wore my steel-toed brown boots. Clunky, yes, but practical, too, because who knows what could happen? I might have to kick him. Plus, the heels were low, which would help me in the event that I had to chase him. Or run from him.

I drank an entire glass of water to drown the butterflies in my stomach.

It did not work.

Next I put on some lip gloss, just because I had time to kill. (That's what I told myself, anyway.)

Then I glanced in the mirror and wiped it off because it looked too shiny.

I pulled my hair into a ponytail and took it down and brushed it out and pulled it back up again.

"You look good," said Finn as he walked into the room. The rare compliment. "But why bother when you don't even like him?"

"Cut it out," I grumbled as I tightened my ponytail.

"It looks better down," said Finn as he plugged in the heating pad.

"I never asked you," I said, but I pulled out my ponytail holder and shook out my hair anyway.

Finn buried his face in the heating pad.

"Um, what are you doing?"

"I told you, faking sick." His voice sounded muffled.

"I don't think you have to go to such elaborate lengths for Milo," I said.

A few moments later, Finn tossed the heating pad onto his bed. His hair was mussed and his face bright red. "This is merely practice for future reference."

"Oh."

"Feel my forehead."

I did. "Scorching!"

"Think Mom and Dad would be convinced?" he asked.

"Um, maybe that you're inexplicably sunburned?"

Just then the doorbell rang.

Finn smiled at me. "Be right back!"

Once he was gone I turned back to the mirror and ran my fingers through my hair one last time.

Then I crept into the hallway, hugged the wall, and peered around the corner.

Milo stood in the doorway looking as cute as ever in faded jeans and a brown corduroy jacket over his ripped navy sweater.

"I shouldn't get too close. I might be contagious," Finn said.

Milo shrugged and took a step back. "No worries, dude. We can hang some other time."

"But I feel bad about canceling after you came all the way over here. Want me to see if my sister's free?"

"You mean Maggie?"

I ducked back around the corner, thrilled that he'd remembered my name. And at the same time, annoyed with myself for caring.

"She's the only sister I've got," Finn replied as he turned around and called, "Hey, Maggie. Want to go to a movie or something?"

That was my cue. "What?" I yelled, pretend clue-less. I counted to ten and then headed toward the door. "I thought you were sick. Oh, hi. It's Milo, right? I didn't even hear the bell."

I hated the way my stomach flip-flopped. The way he still looked cute in a manner that no thief ever should. Especially the type who steals adorable dogs.

"Milo and I were supposed to hang out," Finn explained. "But I'm feeling pretty lousy, so I thought maybe you could go instead."

"Oh." I put on my best casual-yet-surprised expres-sion, like I hadn't been getting ready for the last half hour.

"Want to see a movie or something?" asked Milo.

A movie meant sitting in the dark for two hours. Maybe more.

A movie sounded romantic, and if Milo had sug-gested it last week, I'd have jumped at the chance. But tonight I had to steer clear of anything datelike for many obvious reasons.

On the other hand, if we sat in the dark for two hours, we wouldn't have to talk. So yes, a movie sounded like the right thing to do.

Unless we shared a tub of popcorn and both reached for a handful of kernels at the same time and he tried to hold my hand. I saw that move on a com-mercial once.

Or what if I couldn't control *my* hormones and tried to hold *his* hand?

I'd just have to be strong. Avoid any potentially sticky situations. Slimy situations, really, considering I was talking about buttered popcorn and not candy.

Of course, candy would easily solve that problem. I'd get Junior Mints instead.

"Okay, we can go to the movies but I'm not getting popcorn," I blurted out.

Milo smiled. "I wouldn't force you."

"Right. Good. Um, let's go." I pushed past him, pulling my arms in close to my body so we wouldn't touch. Except my shoulder accidentally brushed against his and I felt a little current of electricity shoot through my body. But did it mean I was afraid of him? Or attracted to him? Or both? I couldn't tell. Or maybe I just didn't want to admit the truth.

"You cannot like this guy," I mumbled to myself.

"What's that?" asked Milo, following me downstairs.

"Nothing." I opened the front door and headed outside, jumping to the sidewalk from the third step.

Then I regretted the move, because it probably made me look like a little kid.

Of course, then I regretted having regrets, because why should I care what Milo thought? He's the bad guy.

We started for the Pavilion, which is sixteen whole

blocks away. A fifteen-minute walk if we hurried. That's a long time to spend with someone you should be avoiding.

"So, um, your dog is cute," I said.

"Thanks," said Milo. "She's not mine, though. I was just, uh, walking her for a friend."

Liar! Thief! Creep!

I kept these thoughts to myself.

"What's her name?"

"Bitsy," said Milo.

"Bitsy? Really?" I asked, all the while thinking, How much are you shaking down her owner for? Is a hundred bucks your going ransom rate? Does it depend on the dog? Or the owner?

I just wished I had the guts to ask him out loud. Nancy Drew would've. Of course, Nancy wouldn't have been attracted to Milo in the first place. She's faithful to her boyfriend, Ned Nickerson. And even if Ned weren't around, I'm guessing she'd be into someone more clean-cut—the type of guy who'd wear a cardigan or an argyle sweater-vest.

"Yes, Bitsy. You think I could make that up?" asked Milo.

It made me nervous, how convincing he sounded.

I think even if this were a regular date, I wouldn't have known what to say or how to act. But knowing that Milo was a dangerous criminal made the conversation that much harder.

I wanted to ask him more about Bitsy. Catch him in a lie. But I didn't know where to begin.

"So, um, when did you move to Brooklyn?" I asked instead.

"I've always lived here. Just in another neighborhood, before." Milo kicked a loose stone up the sidewalk and it bounced into the gutter. "My dad and I lived in Williamsburg."

"Why'd you guys move here?"

"We didn't. I did after my dad's girlfriend moved in with him. She and I don't get along so well."

"So you live with your mom?"

"My grandma," said Milo. "My mom died."

"Oh." My heart broke just a little bit. He had no mom. And his dad had shipped him out. He was half an orphan. How sad was that? Could it explain his criminal behavior? Was I being too hard on him? But still, how did that justify stealing innocent dogs? It didn't. The two had nothing to do with each other.

Still, my chest ached just thinking about it.

"I'm so sorry," I said, never knowing what the right thing to say was.

Milo twisted up his mouth and shrugged. "Yeah, it happened a while ago."

Just because something happened a while ago didn't make it any less painful. This I knew. Milo didn't have a mother every single day of his life. I couldn't imagine that. But I didn't say so because I didn't know how to or even if I should. I half wished I hadn't brought up his mom in the first place. But at the same time, I was glad he told me. Not that it explained anything, exactly, but just because it told me more about who he was, or about some part of him, anyway.

We walked to the theater in silence and when we finally got there, Milo asked me what I wanted to see.

We settled on an action film starring this old muscley actor whose name I can never remember. We bought tickets and then candy and the theater dimmed as soon as we sat down.

I didn't offer Milo any Junior Mints and he didn't ask. He wasn't missing much. They were stale and half of them had melted together. Milo's peanut M&M's were probably the better choice. But he didn't offer me any of his candy, either.

The movie had lots of explosions and a car wreck and, at one point, a helicopter crashed into a burning building. The hero survived three stabbings and one gunshot wound and still looked cute—and not even super stressed—while he saved the day. He wore a tank top that got torn but not dirty. It bothered me how his shirt stayed sparkling white, like he'd just pulled it out of the washing machine. If I'd seen the movie with Lucy we'd have laughed about it later.

But when Milo and I stepped outside into the dusky night, he asked, "Want to get some pizza?" all serious.

"No thanks." I faked a yawn and backed away. "I should get going. I've got a ton of homework."

"Want me to walk you?"

"You don't have to," I replied quickly. Then I realized I'd messed up. If I went home now, I'd have wasted the whole afternoon. I still had no idea where Kermit was. Or what Milo had done with the other dogs he'd stolen.

If only I knew how to get him to confess.

Um, good movie—steal any dogs lately?

Oh my, look at the time. So where are you hiding Kermit?

Did you do the science homework yet? And by the way, I saw you steal that adorable golden retriever. Do you enjoy extorting grandmothers?

Accusations don't naturally roll off the tongue. Not mine, anyway.

But I couldn't blow this chance. I needed more time. "On second thought, I'm starving. Let's go to the Pizza Den."

"Cool," he said.

"Cool," I repeated.

And then we walked in silence for a while.

"So what did you think of the movie?" he asked once we got to Seventh Avenue.

I shrugged. "It was okay."

"Yeah, that's what I thought."

We were approaching a dog tied to a parking meter. A scruffy little mutt, part Chihuahua, I think. And Milo stopped to pet it. The dog raised his head, grateful for the attention, with no idea of whom he was dealing with.

Would this be Milo's next victim? I could already see the "Missing Dog" poster in my head.

"Hey, let's go." I grabbed the sleeve of his jacket and pulled without thinking.

Milo looked at my hand and I quickly took it away. "Sorry," I said. "It's just, I can't stay out too late on a school night."

"Right. Well, maybe I'll just hang out here. Make sure his owner comes back. You never know who could come by. It's dangerous, leaving dogs tied up like this."

I stifled a gasp and tried to act normal. "Um, maybe I'll wait with you. Keep you company."

Milo didn't seem to like this idea. "It might be a while, so if you've gotta go . . ."

Obviously he was trying to get rid of me. And I couldn't believe he planned on stealing another dog—practically right in front of me. This was too much. I couldn't pretend any longer.

"I know what you're doing, and you'd better stop!"
I yelled.

Milo blinked, completely stunned. "What are you talking about?"

"I saw you take that golden retriever."

This funny look passed across Milo's face. He seemed plenty surprised, but there was something else in his expression, too. Something I couldn't quite figure out. "Were you spying on me?" he asked.

"No, I just happened to be standing there."

"Where?"

"Around the corner," I said. "Watching."

He grinned. "Uh, I don't have a dictionary on me or anything, but that's pretty much the definition of spying."

"Okay, fine. I guess you could interpret it that way, but that's not the point. You took that dog!"

"Right—and that lady never should've left him tied up on the sidewalk."

"Why?" I asked.

"Because it's dangerous," he said simply.

"It's dangerous because of people like you!" I cried. "And what do you do with all those dogs you've dog-napped, anyway?"

"Wait, you think I've been *stealing* dogs?" asked Milo.

"You just admitted it!"

"No, you're not listening," he said. "I told you I took the dog. I never said 'steal.'"

"Same difference."

Milo shook his head stubbornly. "No, it's not. It's totally different."

Chapter 22

. . .

"Milo's not the dognapper," I blurted out as soon as Lucy answered the door the next day.

Lucy laughed. "Um, what are you talking about?" she asked.

And I couldn't blame her for being confused. Lucy didn't know I'd seen Milo take the golden retriever outside of Key Food on Monday. Lucy didn't even know about Kermit being dognapped. I hadn't told anyone about what had been going on. Not even Finn. So all Lucy knew was that I'd been avoiding her ever since my birthday party last weekend.

But all that had to change because things had just gotten weird.

Um, weirder.

I walked into her house, not waiting to be invited. "Sorry to show up like this, but I had the weirdest non-date with Milo and—"

"You had a date with Milo!" Lucy exclaimed, clapping her hands together.

"It was a nondate."

"Is that even a real word?"

"Don't know, but it should be."

"Well, how would you define it?" asked Lucy.

I thought about this for a second. "It's complicated, but if I were forced to come up with a—"

"Know what? Never mind. Just tell me about Milo." Lucy grabbed my hand and pulled me upstairs. "Come on. My parents are in the kitchen and we need privacy."

Once we got to her room Lucy flopped down on her bed and hugged her knees. "Shoot!" she said.

"Okay, here goes." I sank down into her blue beanbag chair and took a deep breath. "It all started on Saturday . . ."

Ten minutes later, she knew the whole story. From Ivy trying to "borrow" one hundred dollars to our botched attempt at getting Kermit back to me spying Milo taking the golden retriever.

Lucy tilted her head, confused. "But you said Milo wasn't the dognapper."

"He's not. Turns out he only takes dogs for a little while. It's his thing."

"It's his thing?" Lucy glanced at me skeptically. "That doesn't make any sense."

"That's what I thought at first, but then he explained.

Milo thinks it's wrong to leave dogs tied up alone on the sidewalk. So he takes them in order to scare their owners into acting more responsibly."

"That's awful!" said Lucy. "And it's still stealing."

"Right, *technically* yes—Milo does steal dogs. Only not really. Like, when I saw him take that golden retriever the other day? He didn't run off with it. He only hid with the dog around the corner. He taped a warning note to the parking meter and everything. Then, once the owner came back from shopping, he returned her dog."

"What'd the note say?" asked Lucy.

" 'Please be more careful with your dog. If you leave him alone, someone might take him,' " I repeated. "That's his note for boy dogs, anyway. He has a different version for girl dogs. Well, it's essentially the same note, just with different pronouns."

"That's so weird!" said Lucy.

"I think it shows a nice attention to detail. And doesn't it bug you how some people use 'he' and 'his' when really they're talking about boys *and* girls, like as a group? It's so sexist!"

Lucy shook her head. "No, I mean the whole thing is weird. Him taking dogs, even for a little while."

"Weird, yes. But he's trying to do a good thing."

"But why?" asked Lucy.

"Because he doesn't want anyone to suffer the way

he has. He only started this whole crusade last summer, after he lost his dad's girlfriend's dog, Mitsy. Basically, he tied her up outside a deli and went in to buy a drink. And when he got back outside, she'd vanished."

"So Milo's a victim of the dognapper, too?" asked Lucy.

"Milo's the victim of *a* dognapper. I don't know if it's the same one. But I'm thinking no, because Milo never got a ransom note. In fact, he wasn't even living in Park Slope at the time."

"So how'd he get Mitsy back?" asked Lucy.

I blinked back tears. "That's the awful part. He never did!"

"No!" Lucy cried.

I nodded. "Isn't that awful? The whole experience haunts him. Like, he has nightmares about it. But there's nothing he can do. That's what he thought at first, anyway. Then he realized something. He couldn't change the past. Mitsy was gone for good. But he could try to save other dogs by taking them temporarily. He thinks every dog owner deserves a second chance. The one he never got."

"Okay, I kind of get that. But don't the dog owners get mad?" asked Lucy.

"Sure," I said. "And sometimes it backfires, too. One time, Milo told me, he hid with this toy poodle and when the owner came out of the store, he'd forgotten he'd brought her out in the first place. The guy went back to his house to watch a baseball game. Luckily that poodle had tags, so Milo was able to take her home. And once, after he took and returned a giant schnauzer, the owner screamed at him and threatened to call the police."

"I'd be pretty upset if he took my dog," said Lucy. "If I had a dog, I mean. Even if it were only for a few minutes."

"I know, but it's cool that he feels so passionately about the cause."

"I can't believe you went on a date with him and you never even told me," said Lucy.

"It wasn't a date. It was a disaster. And I didn't even tell you the worst part."

"There's something worse than wrongly accusing the guy you've been crushing on of being a thief?" asked Lucy.

"Yup." I nodded. "Much. Finn set up the whole thing. You know, pulled the bait and switch like I did last year with Amber?"

Lucy grinned. "Your brother is such a sweetheart!"

I gave Lucy a sideways glance. "Are you kidding?"

"Um, yeah. Totally."

But for some reason, I didn't really believe her.

"Anyway, Finn told Milo he was feeling too sick to

hang out. Except when we got back to my street, we found him kicking around the soccer ball with Red."

"Oh no!" said Lucy.

"Finn said he made a miraculous recovery, but I don't think Milo believed him."

"Maybe it's good that he knows you like him," said Lucy.

"But I'm not even sure how I feel anymore. And yes, I'm relieved that Milo isn't the evil dognapper behind Kermit's disappearance, but that still means I'm back to square one. Meaning, I have no idea who did steal Kermit."

"But why are you helping Ivy when she's been so awful to you?" asked Lucy.

I frowned. "I'm not helping Ivy. I'm helping her dog."

"And why does Kermit need help?" asked Lucy. "Because Ivy got distracted while shopping?"

"It sounds bad when you put it that way," I admitted. "But lots of people tie up their dogs and leave them alone on the sidewalk. That doesn't mean they deserve to have them stolen."

"Okay, but why is it your job to find him? Is Ivy even helping?"

"I don't know what she's doing," I said with a shrug. "But it's kind of my fault he's still gone."

Lucy shook her head. "You don't know that. And

you were only trying to help. I think it was smart, going with her and trying to spy. Who knows what could've happened if she'd gone alone? Plus, she's the one who got you involved when she tried stealing your money."

"Borrowing," I replied.

"She snuck into your room and tried to take a hundred dollars without asking."

"Well, when you put it that way . . ."

"And maybe Kermit's dognapper had no intention of ever returning him. Maybe they were just trying to get the money all along."

Everything Lucy said made sense, but it didn't change a thing.

"Yeah, but none of that matters because Kermit's still missing. And he's the sweetest dog. I've got to find him."

My brain hurt just thinking about this mess. So I stood up and began counting the parquet tile squares in Lucy's bedroom. And not just counting them—I walked from one end of her room to the other. Each new square was one step.

"What are you doing?" asked Lucy.

"Just walking within the tiles, trying not to step on the cracks. It helps me focus. I do this at home when I'm trying to figure something out."

I'm surprised I was able to admit it out loud. I'd been doing it for years and never told anyone. Even when Ivy and I were BFFs, it was the kind of thing she'd have made fun of me for. But Lucy didn't even blink when I tiptoed across her room.

Five, six, seven, eight. I counted in my head because even Lucy must have had a limit to how much dorkiness she could take in one day.

When I hit twelve I found myself in the center of the room. This made me pause. I looked back at where I'd come from. I'd definitely gone halfway.

But something struck me as odd. I just wasn't sure what.

Lucy pulled out her knitting. "You okay?" she asked.

Too confused, I didn't answer right away.

How could I be halfway across the room at twelve squares? It made no sense. I continued on my way and ended up at twenty-four—at the other end of the wall.

I wondered if maybe I'd gotten distracted talking to Lucy and counted wrong. So I turned around and walked back across the room. This time when I counted twenty-four squares, I knew I hadn't made a mistake.

"What's wrong?" asked Lucy.

"I'm not sure." I walked it a third time and came up with the same number. "There are only twenty squares in my room."

"Twenty squares?"

"The parquet tiles on the floor," I said. "I just counted and you have four more than I do."

"Huh."

I noticed that Lucy was working on the same green and white scarf she was supposed to have finished by last weekend. "You know, maybe you should give that one to Finn."

"No, you were right. He'd just think it was dumb."

"That's not what I said. I just know he wouldn't buy it. I'm sure he'd be flattered if you gave it to him."

Lucy looked up at me. "You think?"

"Yeah, and I'm sorry I got so sensitive about the twin thing. It looks nothing like the scarf you made for me, and I should've known better."

"Well, anyway. I'll probably just put it up on Etsy. As soon as I finish I'm going to try to knit an owl. I found this cool pattern. Hold on, I'll show you." Lucy stood up and walked to her bookcase.

And I continued to stare at the floor.

"Your room is definitely bigger than mine."

"That's impossible," Lucy replied. "Our rooms are identical. All the houses on this street went up at the same time and they all have the exact same layout."

"That's what I thought until just now," I said. "But you have more squares than I do."

Lucy shrugged. "Maybe my squares are smaller, so it takes more of them to fill up the room."

"Maybe," I replied, although I doubted it. They

seemed the same. I lined up my heel at one end and noticed that the tile ended a couple inches past my foot. Just like at home. The squares were the same size. I was almost sure of it. But there was only one way to know for sure. "Can I borrow a tape measure?"

Lucy pulled one out of her knitting bag and handed it over.

I knelt down on the floor and went about measuring. Each square was ten inches exactly. I wrote down the number, not so I wouldn't forget, but so I wouldn't doubt myself later.

Once I finished I snapped the tape measure closed and asked, "Mind if I take this home? I need to go measure my room."

"Okay. But how come?" asked Lucy.

"Long story."

"Does this have anything to do with Kermit?" she asked.

"Not exactly," I said, slipping the tape measure into my back pocket. "Okay, not at all. But it's something I need to figure out."

"What is it?"

I paused before answering, not knowing how much to tell her. Whether the strange but strong inkling I had about what'd been going on in my building could be true. It was too soon to tell, but my suspicions were strong . . . "I can't say right now, but I'll explain later. I promise."

"Okay." Lucy shrugged, dropping the subject.

I gave her a hug and she laughed. "What was that for?"

"Just because," I said. "Thanks for being a great friend. I'm sorry I've been weird about Ivy lately."

"It's no biggie. And honestly? Having you defend Ivy is a lot more fun than listening to you complain about her all the time."

Yikes! "Have I been that bad?"

"Yup," said Lucy. "Well, sometimes, but don't sweat it. Everyone's weird about something."

"That's a pretty good motto," I said. "And I'm hoping my weirdness ends soon."

Lucy grinned. "Me too."

I ran home and measured my room twice. Sure enough, it was more than two feet smaller than Lucy's room. Yet, Lucy was right. Our houses were supposedly identical in shape, size, and layout. Strange. Or maybe it wasn't so strange. Maybe something was actually starting to make sense.

I gazed out my bay window—the one that looked out onto Garfield Place.

I tapped the wall and found it nice and sturdy—almost an entire foot of solid house between the inside and outside walls.

Next I tapped the wall by Finn's bed. It sounded solid, too.

Same with the wall where our desks were.

But the wall on my side of the room? It sounded different. Flimsy. Not exactly hollow, but almost. When I knocked harder, it seemed to vibrate.

It made me think of Easter bunnies. How there's a big difference between a solid chocolate bunny and a bunny shell.

That was my room—three solid walls and one shell. A shell with a sealed-up crawl space door—something I didn't remember ever seeing on any of Lucy's walls . . .

I sat down in the middle of my room, crossed my legs, and rested my chin on my hands.

Something was up. I had no doubt. But my brain felt fuzzy, trying to figure stuff out. So I stood up again and paced across my room, counting the twenty tiles one way and then the other. And then, very suddenly, it all just clicked.

It sounds so simple, but that's really how it happened. Everything came together in an instant—like those Connect the Dots puzzles I was obsessed with when I was younger.

Some of those puzzles have fifteen numbers and some of them have seventy. You trace your pencil from one to two to three and so on, and at first it just looks like numbers on a page. And then numbers with a random squiggly line going through them. Then they become a familiar shape. And, *bam*—in a flash, you know what you're drawing. That mysterious shape is revealed.

It's an elephant!

It's a unicycle!

It's two kids playing in the sand!

In one instant this problem went from scattered numbers to a clear picture, from nothing to something.

I suppose it was there all along, but I only just then figured out how I was supposed to see it.

Isabel disappearing.

Chloe complaining about mice.

Glen's bass and the reverberating E note.

The "sealed-up" crawl spaces.

That tiny door in the basement—the one that led to nowhere. Or so I'd thought . . .

My room looked so much smaller than Lucy's for a reason.

It wasn't just that I shared it with Finn and we had more stuff.

Our room looked smaller because it was smaller.

And it was smaller because it was more than two feet too short!

As for the missing two feet? Well, that explained even more . . .

I raced downstairs and knocked on Isabel's door. Then, too impatient, I used my key and walked inside.

"Hey, Isabel?" I called. "Are you home?"

Isabel stood in her kitchen washing dishes. Her crutches were propped up by the front door, all the way on the other side of her apartment. "In here, dear," she called. "Didn't you already take Preston out today?"

"I did," I replied. "But I need to talk to you about something. Something I should've brought up a long time ago. You know I love taking care of Preston, right? And how, even if you didn't have a bad knee, I'd still walk him all the time? Since he's the closest thing to my own dog that I'll ever have."

"That's so sweet of you to say," said Isabel.

I swallowed. "So, um, can you walk? Because I can't help but notice that your crutches are at the other end of your apartment. And, well, your surgery was a while ago . . ."

Isabel turned off the faucet and looked at me. Then she stared down at her leg. "Well, yes. I suppose my knee has been doing better."

"That's great news!" I said.

"But I'm not faking," said Isabel. "It still gets sore sometimes. In the rain, for instance, and when I've been on the treadmill for too long."

"You still go on the treadmill?" I asked.

"Care for a glass of juice?" Isabel asked, turning to the fridge. "I have your favorite—pear cider."

"No thanks. I actually need to talk to you about something else."

"Oh, I see." Isabel walked (smoothly and unassisted) into the living room and sat down in her easy chair. "Is everything okay?"

I flopped down on the couch across from her. "Yes! I mean, no. I mean, well, it's complicated. But I think I'm getting close."

She tilted her head to one side. "So cryptic."

"Are you, um, looking for something?" I asked. "When you use the secret passage in the building? The one you can enter through that door in the basement, behind the quilt? The one that leads to those sealed-up crawl spaces? Which aren't really sealed up and aren't really crawl spaces, right?"

Isabel looked worried. Or embarrassed. Or maybe both. One thing was sure, though—Isabel looked guilty. And for once, she was completely silent. Also? Her face got really pale, like the time she'd bought the wrong shade of powder but was too stubborn to change it until she'd used it all up.

"You don't have to tell me," I said. "And I'm sorry for bursting in here like this. It's just, well, a lot of things haven't been making sense lately. And when I finally figured out this one thing, I got so excited, but I shouldn't have . . ."

Isabel shook her head. "No, it's fine. You're absolutely

right, Maggie, about everything. You just caught me off guard."

"So what are you looking for?" I asked carefully.

"My money," she replied.

"Your money?" My mind raced, trying to catch up to what she was saying. But it didn't make any sense. "You mean you hid some money and you can't remember where you put it? But you think it's in Glen's or Chloe's apartment? Or in mine?"

"No, I'm looking for the money that my ex-husband John hid. The money I thought he stole when he left me fifteen years ago." She looked up at me with tears in her eyes. "But what I want to know is, however did you figure it out?"

Chapter 23

• • •

I made Isabel a cup of tea to help her calm down, and once she did, I insisted that she tell me her side of the story first.

1) Yes, she could walk. She'd had knee surgery in July—she never lied about that—but she'd recovered in a few weeks. Still, she didn't want anyone knowing how easily she moved around because she didn't want to get caught sneaking into her tenants' apartments.

2) Not wanting to get caught was also why she used the building's secret passageway. As our landlady, she has keys to every front door in the building, but sneaking in through the back bedroom wall was much, well, sneakier. In other words, she knew she could get away with it.

3) Isabel said she needed to sneak around in order to find her missing money. She wasn't interested in other people's stuff. She was merely trying to recover what was rightfully hers.

Here's what happened: when John left Isabel, he stole all of her savings, too. This she'd told me ages ago. But what she never knew was that he felt guilty afterward and decided to return it. Since he felt too ashamed to face her directly, he snuck back into the house—just days after he'd left for good—and hid the money in a safe place. Then he wrote Isabel a letter.

A letter she never opened at the time because she was too heartbroken to read his final words.

A letter she put away and then forgot about because it was buried under a bunch of junk in her back closet.

A letter she only came across last month, while rifling through said closet in search of more jewelry to hock.

"So he told you he returned the money but didn't say exactly where it was?" I asked, just to be clear.

"He told me he left it in our secret hiding place. But that was fifteen years ago! I can't remember where I left the remote control last night. How am I supposed to remember where I used to hide things way back when?"

I handed Isabel her remote, which I found wedged between the couch cushions as usual. "Okay, so I get that's why you were sneaking around everyone's apartments. But it doesn't explain why you had that secret passageway built in the first place."

"That's the funniest thing," said Isabel. "I never did."

This I found hard to believe. "What do you mean?"

"I told you about the famous magician who built this brownstone—The Coney Island Fakir? Well, it seems he had the false wall built so he could do his disappearing act at home.

"It's always been there," she continued. "But I promise you, before I went looking for this money, I'd never snuck into anyone's apartment. It's just wrong and I've felt so bad about it, but I didn't know what else to do."

"It's an amazing story."

"What's amazing is that you figured it out," said Isabel.

"I had plenty of clues," I said. "So it was just a question of recognizing them and sort of . . . connecting the dots."

"How did you do it?" asked Isabel.

"First there was Chloe complaining about mice in the walls. Or raccoons. Something loud and clumsy, she'd said. And you'd acted so insulted. I didn't really get it at the time but now it makes perfect sense. You were offended because, unknowingly, she was calling you a klutz."

"It's hard, stumbling around in a dark, dusty secret passageway," Isabel cried defensively.

"I'm sure it is," I said. "And I never would've given it a second thought if it weren't for Glen complaining about the sound quality in his studio. Glen was describing the room right below mine and Finn's, which is basically identical. I just knocked on all four walls in my room and the one on the left sounded different. Flimsy and hollow. Something that makes sense, considering the little door I found in the basement this weekend. The one that's the size of the 'sealed-up' crawl space in my room."

"I should've put that padlock on ages ago," said Isabel.

"Lucy's house really confirmed it, though. Our rooms are supposed to be identical, and I'd always figured hers seemed bigger because she didn't have to share it. But it turns out it seems bigger because it is—by over two feet, since she has no crawl space."

"Very clever," said Isabel.

"Thanks," I said. "Do you think I can see the note?"

Isabel reached for her crutches.

"It's okay," I said. "You don't need to pretend anymore."

Isabel opened her mouth to protest, but instead she

smiled. "I shouldn't have tried to fool you," she said. "You're too smart."

I shook my head, wishing she were right. But if I were really smart, I'd have rescued Kermit by now. We were running out of time. Ivy's parents would be home in a few days. And her grandma might actually notice he's missing before then.

That reminded me of something. "I think there's something strange going on at that new veterinarian practice," I said.

"I think you're right," said Isabel. "I took Preston to his old vet this morning and he's as healthy as a horse. Not that every horse is so healthy, of course. Have you seen the poor souls pulling carriages in Central Park? It's simply heartbreaking. Anyway, Preston is healthier than them. He hasn't got any sort of heart problem, just some bad breath. But we had his teeth cleaned and the vet gave me some plaque-busting doggie mints, and—"

"That's great news!" It wasn't until I said the words that I realized how worried I'd been. "This whole thing with Preston really frightened me."

"I know, it's a huge relief," said Isabel. She handed me a thin yellow envelope. "And you've done so much for me already, Maggie. I hate to ask for another favor, but do you think you might be able to figure this out? I feel so foolish for not reading this sooner . . ."

"It's not your fault," I said. "Who puts cash in hiding places?"

"John, apparently," Isabel said with a sigh. "I can't believe how long I've been angry with him. He still left, of course. Still robbed me of the life I was supposed to have. But he didn't take everything, like I'd thought. And I've wasted so many years being bitter."

"It's good that you know now."

"Now that it's too late," said Isabel.

"It's never too late."

"Maggie, he's dead."

"Oh no!"

Isabel blew her nose loudly. "It happened months ago. I read the obituary. Never in my life did I think I'd have to read about John's death in the newspaper."

"I'm so sorry."

Isabel shrugged weakly. "It happens," she said. "Of course, now I may never find the money, since I'm out of places to look. And anyway, it's pretty much too late. My home has been carved up into apartments. I've been forced to sell most of my jewelry. And forget about the travel. The parties. All the years I've missed. And now I'm an old woman."

"You're only fifty."

Isabel dabbed the corners of her eyes with a handkerchief. "Thank you for humoring me, dear. But since

I've come clean about everything else, well, we both know that I'm well over fifty."

"So quit pretending," I said, and then I studied the note.

> Dear Isabel,
>
> I'm so sorry for the pain I've caused you. Please know that this was unavoidable. You have done nothing wrong. It's all me. I am weak but I'm no thief. I've returned your money and I'm sending you a thousand apologies for all the pain and distress I've caused. I didn't mean to fall in love with someone else. These things just happen. Our love burned strong, as bright as fire. But all fires fade and turn into ash. Well, that's it. I've now found a new spark. And speaking of which—you'll find your savings in an envelope in your favorite hiding spot. Please forgive me but I couldn't bear to face you in person. I am a coward and you're probably better off without me.
>
> I hope you can cherish the good times. I know I will. And it's just a sad reality that all wonderful things must come to an end.
>
> With fond memories,
> John

Isabel looked over my shoulder and asked, "Did you get to the part where he claims I'm better off without him? Like he'd done me a big favor by leaving me for another woman!"

She blew her nose again. Loudly.

I didn't answer her because I was too focused on the letter. "You definitely had a favorite hiding spot?" I asked. "He didn't make that up?"

"I've had lots of favorite hiding spots," said Isabel. "And I've been to all the ones I can remember. I've searched this house high and low: the secret passageways, the safe on the second floor, the trick bookcase in Glen's living room, the—"

"There's a trick bookcase in this house?" I asked. "How cool!"

Isabel smiled. "There are lots of cool things in this house, Maggie. You've just got to look closely. And I have. It seems that the one thing this house doesn't have is my money. I'm wondering if John changed his mind and decided to keep it after all. Perhaps he even sent a letter in retraction and I'll find that in another fifteen years."

I read the note a second time, this time really studying it.

"It's probably time to give up," said Isabel. "I don't know why I even bothered. I've been fine without the money and I will continue to be fine. I should burn his

note. It's better than dwelling on the past. More honor-
able than searching for something that's maybe not
even—"

"Hold on," I said, interrupting. "I think I know where
it is."

Chapter 24

. . .

Once I thought about it for half a second, John's clues became obvious, but I guess Isabel was too close to recognize them.

So I pointed them out to her. "See how he writes about a spark and fire?"

Isabel nodded. "Yes, so what?"

"And then it burns out."

"Gibberish," said Isabel.

"No, I think there's more to it. I think it's a clue. He's not just talking about your romance—or not *only* talking about that. It's a metaphor."

Isabel sniffed. "I'm not really following."

"Think for a second. He's dropping hints." I read what I thought was the most important line out loud: "'All fires fade and turn to ash.'"

"I still don't see it," said Isabel.

"Then answer me this—where else do you find

ashes but in a fireplace? And considering that the ones in *this* house are no longer functional . . . where better to hide something important?"

Isabel grabbed the letter and scanned it. "There are fireplaces on all four floors. Can you tell which one he meant?"

"No, but there's only one way to find out."

We checked Isabel's first, but it wasn't there. "I suppose that would have been too easy," said Isabel, frowning into her empty fireplace.

"You're right," I said. "And it can't be in mine, either, because Finn and I use our fireplace to hide stuff. So let's try Glen's."

"All right." Isabel stood and lifted up one of the couch cushions.

"What are you doing?" I asked.

"Looking for the key to that padlock I put on the basement door. I know I put it under a cushion somewhere. Or did I hide it in a kitchen cabinet?"

"Um, I think maybe we're better off using the front door," I said.

"Oh, okay." Isabel blushed. "I suppose I've done enough sneaking around for this lifetime."

Isabel was so excited, she beat me up the steps. We knocked on Glen's door, but he didn't answer.

"I suppose he's not home," Isabel said, and she

turned to me with a gleam in her eye. "Are you sure you don't want to sneak in through the wall? It's kind of fun."

"It's tempting," I said. "But let's try Chloe's place first."

We went downstairs and tried Chloe, who was at home cooking chili. "Can I help you?" she asked, answering the door in a gravy-stained apron.

"Isabel lost something," I said. "A long time ago. And we think it might be in your faux fireplace. Mind if we check it out?"

"Um, I guess not," said Chloe. She stepped aside so we could go in. "Good thing I just cleaned up."

I couldn't tell if Chloe was being sarcastic or not, but her apartment looked pretty messy to me. We had to step over piles of books and a couple of electric guitars on our way past the living room. And Isabel tripped on a drumstick in the hallway, but luckily I caught her before she fell.

When we finally got to the fireplace in Chloe's bedroom, Isabel knelt down in front of it.

"It's painted shut!" she cried, shaking the handle.

"Let me try." I turned the handle and banged the upper left-hand corner, but the door didn't budge. "Um, do you have a chisel I can borrow?" I asked Chloe. "And a hammer?"

She tilted her head and stared. "But I just painted that last week."

"It's an emergency," I said.

"I'll pay to have it repainted," said Isabel. "And if Maggie's hunch is correct, it won't even be an issue."

Chloe sighed and untied her apron. "Okay then. I'll get the tool kit."

A moment later, I was banging away at the chisel, carefully so as not to damage the door (or my fingers). The seal broke pretty quickly, and the thick red layer of paint peeled away, revealing layers of blue, green, and gray. I chipped harder and the flakes scattered to the floor like confetti.

"You sure you know what you're doing?" asked Chloe, staring down at the mess.

"Um, not exactly," I said as I turned the handle and pulled. The door was jammed, of course. I gritted my teeth and yanked harder. The door swung open with a loud creak.

"Well done!" Isabel clapped.

"Let's not speak too soon," I said, reaching into the cold, dark space. I felt something lumpy stuck to the top of it—a large envelope of some sort. I pulled it free. It was covered in ash and stuffed full of something. I handed it to Isabel, figuring it was hers to open.

She peered inside and gasped, hugging the envelope to her chest. "Oh my."

"Don't leave us in suspense," I said.

With tears in her eyes, Isabel nodded. "It's there. I'll need to count it, but from the looks of it, well, John wasn't as bad as I'd thought."

"Um, what's going on?" asked Chloe.

"It's a long story," I replied, sitting back on my heels. "But let me put it to you this way: we just solved your mouse problem."

Chapter 25

• • •

As I lay in bed that night, I thought about Isabel's life and how it linked to mine in ways I'd never before realized. If she'd found her money fifteen years ago, or if John hadn't taken it from her in the first place, she never would've had to divide her brownstone into four apartments.

That meant my family wouldn't live here. We'd be in some other building—probably far from Garfield Place—and my life would be completely different. I'd never have known Isabel, or Preston, either. And with no dog to walk, Parminder never would've mistaken me for a dog walker.

Which meant I never would have become a dog walker. I'd just be plain old Maggie Brooklyn—a twin with a not-so-secret crush, three great friends, and one frenemy.

Or maybe not even that. My parents might have moved to an entirely different neighborhood. Then I'd never have even known Ivy or any of my real friends.

It was crazy to think about how much of what really mattered—all the important stuff—kind of happened at random.

My life as a giant Connect the Dots, a picture in perpetual motion.

But Isabel *had* rented my family an apartment and here I was, wasting time marveling over what could've been and not coming any closer to finding Kermit.

I walked my dogs as usual over the next couple of days, and I noticed some ominous new signs around the neighborhood. A yellow Lab puppy was taken from outside the Tea Lounge on Union Street. Someone stole a Rhodesian ridgeback from the corner of Fifth Avenue and Second Street.

Meanwhile, the days were getting shorter. All the telltale hints of summer—joggers in tank tops, sunbathers on the Long Meadow, kids tearing through sprinklers—had disappeared. Tank top by tank top. Blanket by blanket. Splash by splash . . .

Even the dog beach got less popular—something that seemed eerily foreboding but was probably just a sign of the season. Still, it left me feeling prickly. Restless, too.

Something had to be done—soon.

Discovering the secret passageway in our building, decoding John's note, and tracking down Isabel's life savings—it made me realize something. I'd already solved a bunch of mysteries without even trying very hard.

That meant I could track down Kermit, too. All I had to do was work harder. Somehow flip the metaphorical switch in my brain from stalled to overdrive. I started by making a list of what I already knew.

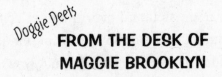

FROM THE DESK OF
MAGGIE BROOKLYN

1) Milo is innocent. Kind of. He doesn't know anything about Kermit, anyway.

2) Jane might be guilty, but if so, she isn't working alone.

3) Dr. Reese tried to operate on Preston for no real reason.

4) Beckett's dog, Cookie, died in surgery. Or so Dr. Reese claimed…

5) According to Beckett and his mom, Cassie's dog, Bean, looks exactly like Cookie.

Meanwhile, I'd never even laid eyes on Cassie, although I'd been walking her dog for almost a month. She'd never returned my call from last week. Was it because she was hiding something? I had to find out, so I picked up the phone and dialed her number. As luck would have it, I learned that Cassie's cable was out. She told me she'd be home the next day waiting for the repairperson.

As soon as school got out, I headed to her apartment.

When Cassie opened the door, I noticed not just her but the brand-new, larger-than-life portrait of Bean hanging on the wall behind her. In it, Bean was chilling out in a pile of leaves, looking peaceful and even friendly, wearing a bubblegum pink coat with a matching bow.

"Do you like it?" Cassie asked.

"It's something," I said to be polite. "I'm Maggie, by the way."

"I figured." Cassie smiled to reveal dimples as she shook my hand. She was pretty—short and chubby with curly red hair and large green eyes. "It's nice to finally meet you in person."

"You, too."

"Isn't it amazing?" she asked, pointing to the painting. "I found this artist online. She works out of Montana and had to paint from pictures, but she really captured Bean's essence, I think."

If she really wanted to capture Bean's essence, she probably should've painted a picture of Bean with someone's pant leg between her teeth, but I kept this observation to myself.

Obviously Cassie loved her dog to the point of being oblivious to her flaws. It was sweet.

"I almost went with a picture of Bean on a blanket in the sand with the ocean behind her. But the last time I took Bean to Coney Island she bit a lifeguard, so I don't think she has the best associations with the beach," she went on.

Just as I'll bet half of Brooklyn has bad associations with Bean, I thought, and since she expected me to say something, I told her I liked the fall leaves. "It's very, um, seasonal."

"So true," said Cassie. "Maybe I should have one made for the winter, too. You know, Bean playing in the snow."

"Does she like the snow?" I had a hard time imagining Bean liking anything.

"I don't know. This will be our first winter together. But I do look forward to buying her a winter wardrobe. Do you think she looks better in red or pink?"

"Um, I haven't given it much thought, but why go with a solid? I have a friend who's an amazing knitter. I'll bet she could make Bean a lovely striped sweater."

"A custom outfit," said Cassie. "That's a fabulous idea! I like the way you think, Maggie. In the meantime, can you take Bean out? It would be just my luck to leave and miss the cable guy, when I've been at home waiting all day."

"Of course," I said. "That's why I'm here!"

"I'll get her new leash." She opened up the closet, rifled through a pile of bags on the floor, and handed me a garish purple thing. "Isn't it cute?"

"Adorable." I clipped the leash to Bean's collar, ignoring the slight snarl on her lips. "Hey, I was wondering about something . . ."

"Are you going to ask me why I'm obsessed with my dog?" asked Cassie. "I know it's a little weird. My boyfriend broke up with me and I bought her a week later, but I don't think those things are necessarily related. You know?"

"No, that's not it," I said, although that kind of explained a lot. "You mentioned you haven't had Bean that long, so I was wondering, when did you get her?"

"It'll be a month in three days," she said. "Which reminds me, I'm throwing her an anniversary party and you're invited. Your dog, too."

"I don't have a dog."

"You don't? That's so sad!" Cassie cried. She really seemed upset by the news.

"My brother's allergic, but it's no biggie, because I'm used to it. Not having a dog, that is. That's why walking them is so much fun. Plus, our landlady has a dog that I help take care of and he feels like mine."

"But still . . ."

"Where did you find Bean?" I asked, finally getting to the point.

"From a local breeder," said Cassie.

"Do you remember the name?"

"I think so." Cassie squinted, like she was struggling to think. "Bertha something."

"Not Brenda?" I asked.

"Yes." Cassie snapped her fingers. "Boutique Breeds by Brenda. I don't know how I could've forgotten."

Just hearing the name out loud gave me the chills. It struck me that Cassie got her dog very soon after Beckett's dog, Cookie, went to the farm. I already suspected Dr. Reese of something fishy. Could her twin sister be involved, too?

"What's Brenda like?" I asked.

"Don't know. I never met her," Cassie replied.

"So she wasn't there when you got Bean?"

"Bean was delivered by messenger, because Brenda doesn't have an actual storefront in Brooklyn."

"So how did you find out about her?"

"I saw a flyer hanging up at a pet store. Beastly Bites on Seventh Avenue? I went in there to buy a dog but it turns out they just sell food and supplies. Not actual animals, unless you count the frozen mice they sell as snake food. I'm not really sure—"

"So you saw the flyer?" I asked to get her back on track.

"Yes." Cassie nodded. "On the bulletin board by the front. And I called the number. Brenda answered and I asked her what kinds of dogs she had and she asked me what kind of dog I wanted and I told her a Maltese. And she said I was in luck because they were expecting a bunch of Maltese puppies the following week."

Cassie was so sweet and sincere—a true animal lover. I'd crossed her off my list of suspects almost as soon as I'd met her, but her story still sounded suspicious. "Did you ever speak to Brenda again?" I wondered.

"Sure," said Cassie. "I called her as soon as I found out Bean wasn't actually a puppy."

"What?" I asked.

"At her first exam, my veterinarian told me she was at least a year old, so I called Brenda to get the story. Brenda was as shocked as I was. She said I could return the dog for something else, but she didn't have any other Maltese puppies in stock and she didn't know when more would arrive. And of course, I'd never think of exchanging Bean. I just wanted an explanation."

"Which she couldn't give you."

"Right," said Cassie. "It's a mystery. But like I said,

Brenda gets her dogs from breeders all over the country, so I figured it was an innocent mistake."

"Uh-huh." I didn't say so, but it sounded to me like
Brenda was the opposite of innocent.

Chapter 26

◆ ◆ ◆

Bean and I did a quick loop around the block. After dropping her off, I ducked into Beastly Bites and spotted the pink flyer immediately. BOUTIQUE BREEDS BY BRENDA was printed across the top in bold black letters. I looked around to make sure no one was watching, then ripped it off the wall and stuffed it in my pocket. After buying some extra poop bags and dog biscuits, I headed out.

Since I was so anxious to continue investigating, I took Milo and Preston for short walks. And when I finally got home, I found Finn and my parents in the living room.

"What's everyone doing here?" I asked.

"I left the office a bit early but it's already past six," said Mom.

"So sorry," I said, glancing at my watch for the first time all day. Luckily I was only ten minutes late, and no one seemed to mind so much.

"Could you set the table for dinner?" asked Dad.

"Sure, in a minute. I just need to make a quick phone call first."

Before I could make it to the cordless, I noticed Finn reading what looked like some sort of invitation.

"What's that?" I asked.

"Here, it's for you, too," said Finn, handing it over.

It was from Isabel and written in fancy calligraphy.

Please join me downstairs for cocktails and light hors d'oeuvres at half past seven tonight. I've had tenants living under my roof for almost fifteen years and I've never had you all over. I'd like to change that. And please arrive promptly. I'm sorry for the short notice, but I have some very big news . . .

Ciao,

Isabel Rose Franini

"She's having a party?" I asked.

"It looks that way," Mom said. "Which is so nice."

"As long as she doesn't talk about Nathan Lane the whole time," said Dad.

"Or how she turned down that big role on *Charlie's Angels* because television was beneath her," Finn added.

"I've never heard that one," said Mom.

"Really?" we all asked.

She grinned and shook her head. "Man, are you all gullible."

I stared at the invitation, tracing the calligraphy with one finger. It seemed so elegant, so reminiscent of how Isabel used to live. When she had a ton of money. Before she had to carve up her house into rental apartments.

And that's when this horrible thought occurred to me. Isabel was rich again, which meant she didn't need us as tenants. Because once more, she could afford to live in her brownstone by herself.

What if this party was just an excuse to gather us all together and tell us in one fell swoop that we had to move out immediately?

Could she do that? Would she do that?

Isabel was so nice. Reasonable, too. Well, reasonable in some respects. So I was sure she'd give us notice. But how much? And more importantly, where were we going to live?

As much as I wanted to run downstairs and ask Isabel what was up, I couldn't. There were more important things to take care of. So I headed to my room and called the number on the flyer.

"Boutique Breeds by Brenda," the woman who answered the phone said in a singsongy and familiar voice.

"Can I speak to, um, Brenda, please?"

"This is she. Who's calling?"

Good question. One that threw me more than it should have. I coughed to stall, and then I blurted out the first name I came up with. "Um, my name is Kir—Kirsten. And I'm calling about a dog."

"Oh good. What kind would you like?" Brenda asked.

"What kinds do you have?" I asked.

"Lots of breeds. Tell me what you're interested in and I'm sure we can arrange something." It was just like Cassie had said.

"Well, I'm not really sure what I want. I think I'd rather pick out a dog in person, so if you give me your address I can drop by."

"Oh no. We don't work that way," Brenda explained. "I'm more like a broker who works with many different breeders. All our pets can be delivered to your doorstep. No fuss, no muss. Do you have an idea of what you want, because I might have it in stock. If not, I'll find it for you within days."

"Days?"

"Sometimes sooner," said Brenda. "It depends on what's around."

I gulped. "And you can get *any* dog?"

"Pretty much. It's just a question of time."

"That's amazing. How do you do it?"

The woman ignored my question. "We seem to have

a lot of large dogs in stock right now. There's a gorgeous collie, a cute little Lab puppy, and a Rhodesian ridgeback who's almost fully grown. Also, I'm expecting a French bulldog any day now."

I covered my mouth to keep from gasping out loud. The breeds she was referring to all had gone missing. And if she was expecting a French bulldog, well, that meant she must be plotting her next crime . . .

"Hello?" she asked.

I almost said I'd like all three. If I bought everything she had, I could return the animals to their rightful owners. But that would probably get expensive. I didn't know if I even had enough money for one dog. Plus, this didn't solve the biggest problem. It wouldn't stop Brenda from stealing again.

"What if I'm not looking for a pure breed? What if I'm looking for a mutt?" I took a deep breath, almost scared to say what I said next. But this was my only chance. So I described Kermit. "Do you have a black-and-white Lab-Dalmatian mix? Something big, with scruffy fur and a few spots? Maybe not even a puppy. Do you have a dog that's a few years old? That's what I'm really looking for."

My question was met with silence.

"Hello?" I asked.

"Who is this?" Brenda demanded.

"Who's this?" I replied.

"You'll never know," she said before hanging up.

We'll see about that, I thought as I pressed redial. Brenda didn't pick up—not that this shocked me.

As I listened to the phone ring and ring and ring, I realized I'd finally figured it out. Brenda had stolen Kermit and the other dogs, too.

And I was pretty sure I knew where she kept them.

Chapter 27

◆ ◆ ◆

I called Lucy as soon as I finished dinner that night. "Ever knit a doggie sweater?" I asked.

"Um, no. How come?"

"I think I found you a client."

"Cool, thanks!"

"Well, don't get too excited. You might feel differently once you actually meet this woman's dog."

"Any customer who's not my grandma is definitely someone I want to work with," said Lucy.

"Hey, how hard would it be for you to sneak out of your house at ten thirty tonight?" I asked.

"Not very hard. My parents will both be at the Manhattan restaurant and the babysitter is usually asleep on the couch by nine."

"Perfect! Do you mind helping me out? I think I know where Kermit is, but I can't spring him by myself."

"Sounds like an adventure," said Lucy. "I'm in!"

"Great. I'll see you tonight."

"Wait, where are we going?"

"You'll see," I replied.

As soon as I hung up I glanced at my watch. It was seven thirty—way too early for the second phone call I had to make. But just in time to hear Isabel's news . . .

I headed into the living room. "Is everyone ready to go?" I asked.

"The kitchen still needs to be cleaned up," said Mom. "But you and Finn go downstairs. Your father and I will take care of that."

"We will?" asked Dad, looking up from his book.

"We will," she told him.

"Cool, let's go," said Finn.

Feeling slightly sick to my stomach, I followed him downstairs. Some peppy jazz music blared from Isabel's apartment, and since the door was already open, we let ourselves in.

Isabel stood in her entryway, wearing the ring I'd found for her last week and a long baggy dress that could only be described as loud and peacocklike. It even had feathers on it. She'd gotten a sleek haircut, had dyed her hair a deeper shade of purple, and had traded in her simple wire-framed glasses for some cute chunky ones with bright red frames.

"Finn and Maggie, so lovely to see you. Come in, come in!"

Isabel raised the pink drink in her hand. "This is the most scrumptious watermelon margarita I've ever tasted. Would you like one? I mean, without the alcohol, of course."

"Have any soda?" Finn asked.

"In the kitchen. Help yourself." Isabel pointed. "And what about you, Maggie?"

"What's the big news?" I asked, even though I was fairly certain I knew. I just needed to hear it from Isabel herself.

But rather than tell me, she laughed and put her arm around me. "My, aren't you an anxious one tonight."

"A little," I admitted. "So what is it?"

"I'd prefer to wait until everyone gets here," said Isabel. "So relax, have some food."

"I'll pass." I felt too nervous to eat. At least until I saw the delicious-looking spread in the dining room. Three trays piled high with cheese, crackers, fruit, hummus, pita bread, quesadillas, empanadas, and guacamole. It was the chocolate cupcakes that made me change my mind, though. "I guess a small bite won't kill me," I said as I headed to the dessert end of the table.

Just then Glen knocked and walked inside. He was dressed in his cycling gear again, and he had his bike propped up in the hallway outside. "Hello, Ms. Franini," he said with mock formality and a real bow.

"Oh hi, Glen," Isabel said dryly, looking him up and

down with a not-exactly-thrilled expression on her face. "I suppose I didn't mention anything about a dress code for tonight."

Glen smiled. "Just be glad I didn't come over *after* my ride."

"Good point," said Isabel. "And what do I care! Why, you should've seen some of the outfits my old friends used to wear. Come in, come in, and have some food."

He walked inside and Chloe followed him.

My parents showed up just a minute later. That meant everyone was here. I wished she'd just tell us the news already. The suspense was killing me!

Everyone was having so much fun hanging out, talking and laughing, eating and drinking. No one had any idea we'd soon be turned out. No one, that is, but me.

After ten minutes had passed, I couldn't stand it any longer, so I pulled Isabel away from her conversation with Chloe and said, "Everyone's here, so can you make your big announcement?"

"Oh, there's no rush," said Isabel. "My plans aren't definite and I still have plenty of things to iron out."

That made sense. She'd probably have to hire a whole construction crew to turn her brownstone back into a single house. Still, evicting all her tenants would have to happen early in the process. Our days were numbered . . .

"Just promise me you'll give us all plenty of notice, okay?"

Isabel blinked at me in confusion. "Notice? Well, I don't see why it should matter much to you."

I couldn't believe she was being so heartless. "I've lived here my whole life," I cried. "Of course it matters!"

"But I'll only be gone for half the year," said Isabel.

"Wait. What?"

"I should ask you the same question," she replied. "What are you talking about, dear?"

"Aren't you kicking us out so you can have this whole brownstone to yourself again?"

Isabel gasped and clutched her chest, splashing her drink in the process. (Although she didn't notice, and the stain got lost in the swirled pattern of her dress within seconds.) "Of course not! Why would I do that?"

"Because you can afford to, and because you always complain about how you're crammed into such a small apartment."

"I'm an old woman," said Isabel. "Why ever would I need so much room?"

I couldn't answer that, but I still had so many questions. Namely, "Where are you going, then?"

"Paris!" Isabel said, waving one hand through the air. "I've rented a lovely flat and I figure I'll spend six months there and six months at home. That's this year, anyway. Maybe I'll try Rome next, or perhaps Buenos Aires. I've never even been to South America. And then there's Bali. There are so many places I'd like to see and so little time . . ."

"But what about Preston?"

"He's coming, too."

"Oh." I tried not to look disappointed. I knew this was good news for Isabel and for all of us tenants. But hiding my feelings was impossible.

Isabel put her arm around me. "I'm sorry, Maggie. I know you'll miss him. But you have other dogs to walk and a whole business to run. Not to mention school, your family, and your friends . . ."

"It's true," I said. "Just, will you promise to send me a postcard?"

"Of course!" said Isabel.

"And pictures of Preston eating croissants?"

"It would be my pleasure," she replied.

I took a deep breath, hoping she'd still be agreeable when I brought up my next—and more urgent—request. "There's one more thing. Do you think I could borrow Preston tonight? Just for an hour or so. Maybe at around . . . ten thirty?"

"Well, I suppose so. But whatever for?" asked Isabel.

"Um, I can't really say, but it's important. And he'll be safe. I promise."

Isabel looked at me carefully. "So mysterious."

"I'll tell you all about it later, okay?"

"Okay, it's a deal," said Isabel. "On one condition. You've assured me that Preston will be safe, but can you say the same thing for yourself?"

"Absolutely," I said with a nod. My voice didn't even waver.

If only I felt as confident as I sounded . . .

Chapter 28

◆ ◆ ◆

The party had ended two hours ago but my night was just beginning. At twenty past ten I took the phone into the bathroom—the only place I could find some privacy—crossed my fingers, and dialed a number I hoped I'd never need again.

"Is this Dr. Reese?" I asked as soon as someone picked up. I felt so legitimately panicked I didn't even have to pretend to act scared.

"Yes, who's calling?" asked the doctor.

"It's me, Maggie Brooklyn. We spoke last week about Preston, my friend's Irish wolfhound?"

"Oh yes, of course, the dog that needs heart surgery. Is he okay? I never heard from you and I've been worried."

"That's why I'm calling." I gripped the phone tighter. "Preston isn't doing so well and I think you were right.

I think he needs surgery and I hope it's not too late. Can I bring him by now?"

"What time is it?" asked Dr. Reese.

"It's almost ten thirty," I squeaked, hoping this would work. Ivy's parents would be home in the morning. Ivy said if I didn't find her dog, she'd ask Milo out first thing. But that's not why I needed to act now.

I figured if I caught Dr. Reese off guard, really surprised her, I'd have a better chance of getting her to confess. And my plan seemed utterly foolproof, but the silence on the other end of the line made me nervous. "Dr. Reese? Are you still there? I wouldn't be calling if this weren't urgent. So can I bring him in?"

"Yes, of course," Dr. Reese said. "Meet me at my office. I must warn you, though, the fee for emergency surgery is higher."

"Isabel doesn't have a problem with that," I bluffed, amazed at the gall of this so-called doctor. "We're just so worried about poor Preston. Do you think you can make him better?"

"Well, I can't make any promises, but I'll see what I can do. Can you meet me at my office in ten minutes?"

"Absolutely!" I cried. "Thank you. Thank you so much. We'll be right there."

I hung up and crept back into my room.

Finn was already asleep—or so I thought. After I

tiptoed across the floor and stuffed some pillows under my quilt, he shot straight up in his bed and asked, "Is it time?"

I jumped. "Oh, you scared me. I thought you were asleep."

"Nope." Finn pulled back his covers and swung his feet to the ground. He was fully dressed—already in sneakers, even. "So, what's the deal? Where are we going?"

"*We're* not going anywhere," I said. "I have some important business to take care of and I was hoping you could be my cover."

Finn shook his head. "Forget it. I'm tired of being your cover. It's boring. If you're going to rescue Kermit, I want in."

"How did you know?"

"I talked to Lucy," said Finn.

"When?"

"We talk all the time." Finn looked at his watch. "So let's go. She's probably outside already and we shouldn't keep her waiting."

"Finn, you can't come. You're allergic to dogs."

"Hardly."

We both knew this was a lie, but there wasn't enough time to argue.

"Fine, hold on a second." I took my schoolbooks out

of my backpack and loaded it with dog biscuits and spare leashes.

"Ready?" asked Finn.

I pointed to his bed. "What about your body double?"

Finn lined up his pillows on his bed and tucked the blanket around them.

"You're skinnier than that."

"Either way, this would never fool them. If they come in, we're caught," he said, but he still tucked the blankets tighter and added a soccer ball in place of his head.

Then we crept out through the dark and silent apartment.

"We've gotta get Preston," I whispered once we made it downstairs. I let myself into Isabel's place using my key, and I leashed up her dog. Then the three of us walked to Lucy's. As planned, she was waiting on her front stoop.

"Finally," she said, standing up and petting Preston.

"I would've been here sooner, but someone blabbed to Finn!" I said.

"Whoops, sorry!" Lucy raised one hand to her lips as if caught. Or was she merely trying to hide her smile? I couldn't tell. "I figured we could use the backup. You're not mad that I told him, are you?"

"It's fine," I said. "Let's go."

We headed for Sixth Avenue. By day, the sidewalks of Park Slope are crowded with kids and moms and dads and nannies and strollers. I figured they'd be empty now. The sun had set and the stores were closed. Why be out? But I was wrong. It seemed as if the daytime crowd had switched places with a whole new breed of humans. Now the sidewalks teemed with new life. People I'd never seen before went into bars and restaurants and hung out on street corners. But this put me at ease, because there's nothing eerier than a deserted street.

"So, will you finally fill us in? Why do you think this veterinarian has Kermit?" asked Lucy.

"It's not just Kermit," I said. "It's a bunch of other dogs, too. And I don't even think she's a real veterinarian." I told them about my run-ins with Beckett and his mother. And how I suspected that their dog, Cookie, and Cassie's dog, Bean, were one and the same.

"So you think Dr. Reese pretended that Cookie died in surgery just so her sister could resell her to someone else?" asked Finn.

"Basically," I said. "Through Boutique Breeds by Brenda. A phony dog-breeding business, as far as I'm concerned. She listed pretty much every missing dog in the neighborhood when she told me what was available for sale."

"Kermit, too?" asked Lucy.

"Well, no," I admitted. "But I have a feeling she's got him, too."

"We snuck out of the house because you have a feeling?" asked Finn.

"It's a strong feeling," I told him. "And no one forced you to come."

"Aren't you worried that Dr. Reese might really try to perform surgery on Preston?" asked Lucy.

I bent down and scratched Preston behind his ears. "No, I'd never put Preston in that kind of danger. I'm not going to leave her alone with him for a second. And anyway, she's not going to have the time. As soon as she takes me and Preston back to an exam room, you guys need to sneak inside and track down the missing dogs."

"But what if we can't find them?" asked Finn.

"You'll hear them," I said. "I did when we went in for the exam. That was Dr. Reese's first mistake. She complained that she had no business and her waiting room was deserted, yet I heard a bunch of dogs barking from somewhere inside the building."

"But what if those aren't the right ones?" asked Lucy.

"If not, we're in trouble. But I'm pretty sure I know what I'm doing."

"I hope so," said Finn.

I stopped when we hit Sixth Avenue. "We'll soon

find out. You guys hang back here, okay? Wait about three minutes, then sneak in after me."

"Okay. Good luck," Lucy whispered.

"Thanks!" I replied, hoping I wouldn't need it.

As soon as Preston and I turned the corner, I saw Dr. Reese waiting in front of her office, wearing a white lab coat over her dark suit.

"Thanks for meeting me here," I said, hurrying over. "I'm so worried about Preston."

"You did the right thing," said Dr. Reese. She unlocked her door and walked inside. Preston and I followed, and luckily she didn't try to lock the door behind us.

So far so good.

We went into the same exam room as last time. "Is this where you operate?" I asked.

Dr. Reese ignored the question. "Preston looks even sicker than before. It was dangerous, waiting this long."

"I know. I'm so sorry. Isabel feels terrible. She wanted to get a second opinion and . . ." Suddenly I stopped talking.

Dr. Reese was looking up at me. "Did she get that second opinion?"

"I don't think so," I bluffed, shaking my head. "We trust you." It was hard to say it, but I knew I had to keep talking. Keep Dr. Reese distracted while Finn and Lucy snuck in.

Just then I heard the squeak of the door.

Unfortunately, Dr. Reese did, too. She looked up.

"Windy out, huh?" I asked.

Dr. Reese blinked at me behind her glasses.

"So what's involved in this surgery, exactly?" I wondered.

"Well, I cut him open and repair his heart."

"Uh-huh. And what's your success rate?"

"Well, this surgery is rare," said Dr. Reese. "But I haven't lost any patients yet."

I guess that statement could have been true, depending on her definition of "lost."

Just then I heard a bark. Then another, until soon it sounded like we were in the middle of a dog kennel.

"Excuse me," said Dr. Reese.

"Wait." I grabbed the sleeve of her lab coat. "I have some more questions. Please don't go."

Dr. Reese pulled her arm free. "I really need to go check on my other patients."

"How long will it take for Preston to recover?" I asked, trying to stall her.

"Just a few weeks," said Dr. Reese, her hand on the doorknob. "You'll want to keep Preston quiet. He shouldn't run around until his stitches heal."

"He'll have stitches?"

"Of course he'll have stitches."

"I had stitches once," I said, thinking if I just kept

talking I could distract her. "On my elbow. I fell off my bike into a pile of broken glass. It hurt. A lot. Will Preston be in pain?"

Dr. Reese smiled and walked over to me. "Don't worry so much."

Just then, Finn sneezed. Which would've been bad enough even if Lucy hadn't said, "Bless you."

When we heard Finn say, "Thank you," with crystal clear clarity—even through the door—I knew we were toast.

Dr. Reese flew out of the exam room.

Preston and I followed her down a long, narrow hall and through an open door.

We soon found ourselves in a brightly lit room with Finn and Lucy and seven dogs—Kermit included.

"We've got her!" I yelled.

"What's going on here?" asked Dr. Reese.

"We should ask you the same question!" I said.

"This is a clear case of breaking and entering," said Dr. Reese, pulling her cell phone out of her pocket. "If you kids don't get out of here now, I'm calling the police."

"Don't bother," said Finn. "We already did."

Chapter 29

. . .

"So, can you explain things one more time?" asked Lucy, once Dr. Reese had been arrested and the police had finished questioning us. We were finally on our way to Ivy's with both Preston and Kermit in tow.

"Yeah, my head is still spinning," said Finn.

"That's because of your allergies," I said. "Which I warned you about before you came!"

"Oh, get over it," said Finn. "You should be thanking me, since I'm the one who called the police."

"That was a good move," I said.

"Hello?" said Lucy. "Still waiting for answers!"

"Right. Sorry." I took a deep breath and repeated what I'd already told the police (since they'd insisted on questioning us separately to make sure our stories matched, not believing at first that Lucy and Finn didn't actually know that much). "Dr. Reese is a pretend veterinarian and her whole practice is a total front. She used it in order to get to know local dogs and their owners—essentially to lure in victims. When she examines a valuable purebred dog, she recommends surgery. She later claims that these poor dogs died during surgery, when really she's just pretending to kill them off. Those same 'dead dogs' are later resold through Boutique Breeds by Brenda. Just as I suspected."

"I can't believe that worked," said Lucy.

"But how does Kermit fit into this?" asked Finn. "He's a mutt."

"Right," I said. "Good question. People pay top dollar for purebred dogs and many of them look alike, so it's easy to pull off. But as for mutts? They're too distinct to steal and resell, especially in the same neighborhood. That's why they get kidnapped and held for ransom or stolen for the reward money. Whichever Dr. Reese thinks will work best. On a case-by-case basis."

"Evil twin dog stealers," Lucy marveled. "That's crazy."

"Do you think you'll be able to track down Brenda?" asked Finn.

"I don't need to, because Brenda and 'Dr.' Reese aren't actually twins."

"You told me they looked exactly alike," said Lucy.

"They do, because they're the same person."

"Wait, you're saying she's a fake twin?" asked Finn.

I nodded. "Yup. It's her cover—and a pretty brilliant

one, too. A veterinarian who also sells dogs sounds way too suspicious. But a veterinarian whose twin is a dog breeder? That makes perfect sense. Identical twins who both love dogs decide to work with animals for a living—that's an acceptable backstory. But actually the opposite is true. Obviously this woman doesn't care about dogs at all. People either, or she'd never commit such awful crimes."

"How'd you figure it out?" asked Finn.

I paused before answering because my actual reason sounded silly. Or at least unscientific. In truth, I'd been suspicious ever since I noticed Dr. Reese wore the same shoes as her sister, Brenda. Twins going into similar lines of work made sense. But grown-up twins dressing alike? Forget it! It was too weird.

Of course, there were other red flags I was perfectly willing to talk about. "When I took Preston in to have his nails clipped, I just got this weird vibe from Dr. Reese and the whole office. She worked all alone and told me her receptionist had just quit, but she also said she'd talked to Isabel days before. Most vets don't answer their own phones or make their own appointments. I know because I called around to check. And she was so insistent that Preston needed surgery, when all she did was listen to his heart. It made no sense. At first I took her word for it and panicked, but the more I thought about it, well, Preston seemed so healthy. And after Isabel took him to a different vet, who determined he was perfectly fine? Well, then I knew something was up."

"I wonder how many dogs she pretended to kill," said Finn.

"I wonder how many she stole," said Lucy.

I shuddered. "Let's just be glad she won't be able to do any of it again," I said. And since we were almost at Ivy's, I asked to borrow Lucy's cell phone so I could give her a call.

"Tick tock. You're almost out of time," Ivy said. "You didn't find him, did you?"

"Just meet me outside of your apartment," I said.

"When?"

"Now." I hung up before she could argue with me.

"You should go alone," Finn said. "Lucy and I will hang out here."

"Are you sure?" I asked.

"Yeah, we'll be fine," said Lucy.

"Go ahead." Finn sat on the sidewalk and pulled Lucy down next to him—into his lap, practically.

She giggled.

"Okay," I said, and I walked another half block with Kermit before I saw Ivy's front door open. Then Ivy herself stepped outside into the night. She wore a long purple coat over blue flannel pajamas. Fluffy pink bunny slippers, too.

When Kermit noticed her he whipped his tail back and forth. Then he started barking, so I dropped his leash and he tore down the sidewalk.

"Kermit!" Ivy cried and crouched down to meet him. Kermit jumped on Ivy and licked her face, a frantic and hyper reunion. "I was afraid I'd never see you again!"

"He missed you," I said, once I caught up.

"Not half as much as I missed him!" Ivy wiped the tears from her eyes. "I'll never let him out of my sight again," she promised as she stood up and gave me an awkward hug. "Thanks, Maggie."

"You're welcome."

She let go and took a step back. "So how did you find him?"

"It's kind of a long story." I told her what I could as quickly as possible, since I didn't want to keep Finn and Lucy waiting.

"I can't believe you rescued so many dogs," said Ivy. "That's crazy!"

"Yeah, well, the police are dealing with the others, but I convinced them to let me deliver Kermit to you personally."

"Wow, I'm impressed," said Ivy. "And I'm so glad he's safe."

"Just in time," I said.

"I know. And now my parents will never know a thing!"

"And you can stop torturing me about Milo," I added.

"Huh?" Ivy looked at me, surprised. "You know I was totally joking about that, right?"

"No you weren't."

"I was." Ivy nodded, wide-eyed and innocent. "I'd never do that to you. Not when you've been working so hard. And, um, sorry for everything else, too."

I couldn't tell if she was apologizing for the past two weeks or for the past two years, but strangely, it didn't really matter. It's just who she was. Who she'd become, anyway . . .

"Don't worry about it," I said, and I meant it. I was done worrying.

"Well, you just did me the hugest favor ever, Maggie. And I'm eternally grateful. If there's anything you—"

"Seriously, forget about it." I didn't want to hear it and I didn't need to. So I gave Kermit a final pat good-bye and walked back up the street to Finn and Lucy.

As we headed home I realized something. There are lots of mysteries out there. Some of them I can solve, like tracking down Isabel's cash and finding Kermit and the other neighborhood dogs. And some still left me perplexed:

Why do friendships end?
Will I ever be able to act normal in front of Milo?

And how come my brother and Lucy were acting
so weird around each other?

I figured some answers would come to me, eventually. And some I'd never understand. In the meantime,
I'd just keep walking dogs, knowing that things are
always changing—sometimes for the better and sometimes not.

Chapter 30

• ◆ •

A few days later I ran into Milo at the Pizza Den. He was leaning against the wall and listening to his iPod, as usual. Of course, by now I knew better than to try to talk to him when he had earbuds in.

He noticed me come in, though, and nodded.

I raised my eyebrows at him and gave a half wave. Which was much cooler than actually waving. Or at least it took less effort, and therefore showed less commitment, which translated into nonchalance, which was cool. I think.

When I made it to the front of the line, I ordered my pizza to go.

Once outside, I took a couple of bites, then felt someone tap me on the shoulder. I spun around to find Milo with his earbuds around his neck, both ears free. "Hey, where are you going?" he asked.

"Work. I've got four dogs to walk."

"Four?" asked Milo. "I thought you only had three clients—Preston, Bean, and dog-Milo."

I smiled, flattered that he remembered all the dogs in my life. "I also walk one more now—Nofarm."

"Someone has a dog named Nofarm?" Milo asked.

"Not just someone. It's Beckett. The three-year-old who used to have Bean."

Milo knew the entire story. We talked before science now. After, too, and okay, sometimes during class. He'd forgiven me for accusing him of being the dognapper and I'd sort of forgiven him for his habit of dog borrowing, which he said he might give up soon anyway. Finn told him all about the evil Dr. Reese and how I'd rescued Kermit and six other neighborhood dogs, which impressed Milo. And it also made me realize my brother is not so clueless after all.

"Beckett didn't want Bean back?" asked Milo.

"He did, but his mom decided she'd be better off with Cassie. Beckett was really upset about it, until his parents took him to the BARC shelter in Williamsburg and let him pick out a new dog. He got a mutt this time— a beagle-Lab-collie mix, and she's a total sweetheart. Hasn't bitten anyone yet."

"But why'd he name her Nofarm?"

I grinned. "He has his reasons."

Milo raised his eyebrows as if wanting me to go on, but I didn't.

"Want some company?" he asked.

"I've gotta get to work, remember?"

"I know." Milo stood there as if waiting for something.

"Um, you mean you want to come with me?"

"I could do that," said Milo with an easy shrug. He wore a new sweater—green and gray striped with no holes, just one snagged thread near his right cuff. "I've got nothing else going on right now."

"Wow, thanks."

"No, that's not what I meant," said Milo. "I mean, it would be fun to hang out. If you want to, that is. Or I can call Finn. But maybe he's still sick?"

"Ha, very funny!" I punched him on the shoulder, but not hard or anything.

"Yee-ouch," Milo said anyway, but I could tell he was just teasing.

"Okay, you can come on one condition. You've got to promise me—no dognapping."

"Dog borrowing," Milo said. "There's a difference. And I told you, I'm not doing that anymore."

"Okay, cool. Let's go."

Milo followed me up Garfield all the way to Isabel's.

After Preston, we walked dog-Milo and Bean. Boy-Milo wanted to meet Nofarm, too. So we went to pick her up.

A little while later, we crossed the street to get to

the Long Meadow. We had to move quickly—dodging cyclists, who got as close to us as possible without actually running us down. Trying to edge us out on purpose, because they want you to know that Prospect Park is for them, not for dogs or walkers and especially not for kid dog walkers. But I didn't care. Nothing could spoil this day.

People flew kites. Toddlers ran, screaming—not from anything in particular. Just because toddlers don't need any excuse to run and scream. They just enjoy it.

A soccer game was going on, in full swing. Players running so hard and fast, I felt the ground shake as they sped past. Then the ball got kicked out of bounds. Milo went to retrieve it and threw it back to a familiar-looking blond guy.

"Oh, hey," I said, once I recognized him.

"Hi," he said with a brace-faced smile. "How's your crazy friend with the Muppet?"

I laughed. "Not so crazy anymore," I said, feeling generous. "You just caught her on a bad day. And we found her dog."

"Glad to hear it," he replied before getting back to his game.

"You know that guy?" asked Milo as we continued down the path.

"Yeah, kind of," I said. "It's a long story."

"You seem to have a lot of those."

I shrugged. "It's been that way lately."

I could've explained but didn't want to. Milo didn't need to know everything . . . So I stayed quiet, heading past the dog beach where two pit bulls and a German shepherd splashed through the murky water.

"So, dog walking." Milo looked around. "Who knew? This is kinda fun."

"I know," I said. "I used to walk dogs because it was the next best thing to having my own. But now I think it's better this way. I mean, I still wish I had my own dog, but I feel pretty lucky, getting to spend time with four of them almost every single day."

Milo moved a little closer to make room on the path for a couple pushing triplets in a giant red stroller. The two of us brushed shoulders. "Sorry," he said.

"It's okay."

The spot where we touched felt warm.

Even though the family had passed, leaving the path wide open, Milo stayed close. Not touching me, but almost.

"You know, if you walked a few dogs at once, you could add a bunch of new clients and make more money," said Milo.

"I guess." I shrugged. "But any more might get confusing. I can only keep track of so many house keys. And I don't want to push things with my parents. I'm already lucky they agreed to let me keep this job, since they're so obsessed with me finding enough time for schoolwork."

"Maybe we could join forces," said Milo. "Be a dog-walking duo."

I frowned up at him. His floppy hair was still pretty floppy, his eyes bright—no longer so troubled.

When I didn't answer him he looked away. "Or not." He shrugged, bent down to pick up a stick, and tossed it. "Just something to think about."

"Okay," I said.

"Okay?" he asked.

"No, I mean, okay I'll think about it."

By the time we dropped off Nofarm, the sun had started to set and it was nearly six o'clock. My parents wouldn't want me walking dogs in the dark. Once winter arrived, it would be hard to fit them all in. Of course, Isabel and Preston would be in Paris after the first of the year. But three was still a lot to manage.

Maybe it would be good to get some help, to add more clients.

I glanced at Milo, but only for a quick second, because I didn't want him to think I was checking him out.

The thing is, I really liked him. But did I want to work with him? It seemed like a big commitment. And still kind of soon.

Plus, how could I be sure he wasn't going to have a relapse and fall back into his habit of dog borrowing?

Maybe he'd object to all of Cassie's doggie clothes and decide to teach her a lesson by taking Bean.

Or maybe he'd decide that Beckett's family's tiny apartment wasn't fit for a dog as energetic as Nofarm. Okay, I knew the odds were slim, but you never knew. People are surprising.

Of course, I didn't say any of this out loud because I didn't want to spoil the moment. So we continued to walk in silence, heading off together into the sunset. But not in that "happily ever after" way. I mean, I was happy. And the sun happened to be setting, the sky radiating warm pink and orange light, just like in a painting. Except better because it was real.

I could picture what we looked like from the outside: a girl and a boy walking together. And, well, you know . . .

It's funny how pictures don't necessarily lie, but they don't tell the whole story, either. You really have to look closely. Consider each angle and weigh every possibility before you Connect the Dots.

Because even though on the surface this looked like a happy ending, it wasn't the end. Not by any stretch.

It was only the beginning.

We parted ways at Garfield and I continued walking alone, passing lots of brownstones along the way. Some were reddish brown like mine. And some were white or olive green or blue, and one was even Pepto-Bismol pink. It occurred to me that people lived in every one. People with complicated lives and probably plenty of mysteries, too.

I could do something about that.

Be more than Maggie Brooklyn, Dog Walker.

This was the perfect time to try something new. Turn myself into Maggie Brooklyn, the Dog-walking Detective.

Or perhaps I already had.

Acknowledgments

• ♦ •

Special thanks to my Brooklyn research team of tweens for reading an early draft of this story and telling me which parts had to be cut because they were boring or confusing or just kinda dumb: Megan Superville, Layla Beckhardt, Julia Candea, Sophie Nauman, and Zack Palomo. Megathanks to Laurence Richardson for sharing the ins and outs of dog walking in the Slope.

This book would not exist without Michelle Nagler, editor extraordinaire. Thanks to her and to everyone else at Bloomsbury, including Melanie Cecka, Caroline Abbey, Jennifer Healey, Nicole Gastonguay, Donna Mark, Vanessa Nuttry, Rebecca Mancini, Stacy Cantor, Ben Holmes, Deb Shapiro, Beth Eller, and Diana Blough.

Finally, I'm eternally grateful to Laura Langlie, Coe Booth, Ethan Wolff, Jessica Ziegler, Amanda McCormick, and my incredibly supportive and highly entertaining family: Jim, Leo, Lucy, and Aunt Blanche Margolis.

When movie mania comes to Maggie's neighborhood,
so does a new mystery.

And there's only one super sleuth for the job. . . .

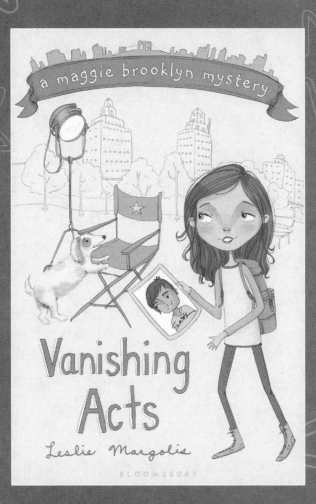

a maggie brooklyn mystery

Vanishing
Acts

Leslie Margolis

BLOOMSBURY

Read on for a sneak peek
of Maggie Brooklyn's next mystery

Not only did my parents sign the release form for me later that night, they also signed a copy for Finn.

Yes, Finn, my brother.

The same brother who thinks Seth Ryan and all Seth Ryan fans are super dorky had volunteered to be an extra in the new Seth Ryan movie.

I asked him why, but "I have my reasons" is all he'd tell me; totally mysterious. I could not figure it out. Not until I found him waiting for me at Lucy's locker after school the next day.

"This is some elaborate plan to make fun of me and my friends, right?" I asked. "You're just hanging around so you can gather material. Make teasing us that much more authentic."

"What are you talking about?" asked Finn.

"Just admit it." I punched him in the arm for even thinking the thought.

"Ow!" said Finn, backing away from me. "Cut it out."

"I think he really wants to be an extra," said Lucy, sneaking up from behind. Her hair was freshly brushed, lips shiny with gloss. She'd changed into her favorite black pants and purple hoodie.

"Oh, you got dressed up for Seth Ryan?" I asked.

"Something like that," Lucy replied. "Let's go."

"What about Beatrix and Sonya?" asked Finn.

"Their plan was to sprint to Second Street as soon as the bell rang," Lucy explained. "So they're probably already there."

As we headed over, Finn asked Lucy, "How was your math test?"

"Good," she replied. "I think. Although last time I thought I did well on a test I barely got a B minus, so who knows."

"That was a killer, though," said Finn. "I'll bet you did great today."

"You're too sweet." Lucy leaned into him and they bumped shoulders.

Forgetting her bizarre behavior, she was right about one thing: Finn was being totally "artificial sweetener"— the kind that makes my teeth ache. Clearly he wanted something. But before I could figure out what that might be, we turned the corner and I forgot all about my brother.

I was too shocked. I'd passed by Second Street a

gazillion times before, but at the moment, I didn't even recognize the place. The entire block had been transformed into a winter wonderland. I'm talking igloos and icicles, twinkling lights and snow people. Like we were in the middle of December—in Alaska. Obviously it was all fake, or at least manufactured. I could hear the hum of three snow machines working overtime.

But the block-long snowstorm wasn't the only thing odd about the scene. All the regular cars parked on the sides of the street were gone, replaced with two crisp rows of silver, futuristic-looking vehicles—something between an army jeep and a semitruck. Except they were propped up by crystal-clear glass so they seemed to float three feet off the ground.

"Does anyone know what this movie is about?" I asked.

"Yeah, I read up on it last night," said Lucy. "It's about a futuristic, post-apocalyptic world where only a handful of teenagers and some grown-up zombies and an army of giant rats have survived, and there aren't enough resources for all three groups, so they're fighting it out, and—oops, my phone is vibrating." Lucy pulled her phone out of her back pocket and read the screen. "Sonya just texted me. She and Beatrix should be right over there." She pointed to a crowd of about twenty people across the street. Beatrix and Sonya saw us and waved.

When we joined them, Sonya said, "Took you long enough!"

I checked my watch. "We came here right when school got out. It's not even four o'clock."

"We've gotta stick to the outside edge so we actually have a chance of being seen on camera," Sonya said.

"And of seeing Seth." Beatrix pointed to one of the trailers parked across the street. "I think that's his dressing room."

"How can you tell which one is his?" I asked, since all six looked identical to me.

"I've seen other people come out of the other five. Plus, it's set back from the street and it's got the most security," she said, and then lowered her voice to a whisper. "Don't look now, but that's the director."

Of course when someone says "don't look now" I have to look, and it's a good thing I did, or I would've missed seeing Jones Reynaldo.

He was tall and skinny with faded black jeans and a matching faded black shirt—like his clothes had spent too much time in the wash. Come to think of it, with his dark, wildly curly hair and his pale skin, it looked like he'd spent too much time in the wash, too—on an extra spin cycle. He wore dark glasses to match the cloudy day.

Jones walked by us fast and stopped in front of a props person (or at least some guy in a black T-shirt that read "Props" on the back).

"What's your name?" Jones barked.

The props guy was skinny and blond, already nervous looking. But once Jones approached, his shoulders seemed to shrink closer to his chest. "I'm Zander?" he asked, like he wasn't exactly sure.

"Zander who lost the inflatable crowd?" Jones asked.

"Yeah—about that. I'm so sorry. I feel terrible."

"Sorry doesn't bring back a crowd of thirty," barked Jones. "Do you know how hard it's going to be to corral real live extras? And are you the guy who built these snowmen?"

Zander looked behind him, as if hoping Jones were talking to someone else named Zander. "Uh, yeah," he said finally.

"And what were your instructions?" asked Jones.

"To build four large snowmen," said Zander.

"Yes—to build four *large* snowmen," Jones repeated. "Then why, may I ask, are there four pathetically tiny snowmen on this set?"

The guy flinched. "Sorry. I'll fix it."

Jones stalked off. Everything about him reminded me of a playground bully, all grown up.

"He's intense," said Lucy.

"That's one way to put it," I replied.

"I read that they wanted him to direct one of the Harry Potter movies, but he turned them down," Sonya whispered.

"Why?" asked Lucy.

"He doesn't do franchises. That's what he told them, anyway," said Sonya.

"Wow!" I replied. This seemed impressive, although I'm not sure why.

Just then, Jones seemed to notice our crowd for the first time. He began heading our way, until a tall blond woman in a short black dress stepped in front of him. "Reynaldo Jones. Is that you?" she asked.

Jones stopped short in his tracks, flinched with his whole body, and looked up at her. "It's Jones Reynaldo, as I think you know. Just like it was me yesterday, Mrs. Weasel. And the day before."

"And I'm Jenna Beasely. Just like I was yesterday, and the day before, and for my whole entire life," said the woman.

So this was my parents' friend. I didn't remember having brunch with her, but she did look vaguely familiar.

"Beasely. Of course. I don't know why I always do that." Jones smirked in a way that said he knew exactly what he was doing.

My friends and I exchanged glances. This was getting interesting.

"What time are you wrapping here?" she asked.

"Impossible to say, since we haven't started shooting." Jones's voice sounded as chilly as the pretend weather. "And I'm sure I don't need to remind you that we have permits to shoot well into the night, and it's only four o'clock now."

"Yes, I'm well aware of your permits," said Ms. Beasely. "And of the fact that you violated the terms last night."

"Well, you didn't have to call the police on us," said Jones.

"Actually, I did. And if you go a minute past eight o'clock tonight I'll shut this movie down faster than you can say 'Brooklyn.'"

"Brooklyn!" he shouted.

"Don't test me!" she warned.

"Just kidding. Sheesh. Where's your sense of humor?"

"I'm much funnier when I'm not kept up all night because of some ridiculous movie shoot," she argued.

"It wasn't all night," said Jones. "And we're allowed to work until eleven tonight. We just got an official extension."

"Says who?"

"The mayor's office." Jones smiled smugly, as if daring her to disagree.

Jenna pulled out her cell phone. "I'll call right now to verify that."

Jones trembled in an exaggerated way and held up his hands. "Oooh, she's got a cell phone. How frightening!" he replied sarcastically.

Meanwhile, Jenna punched in the numbers with such force I feared she'd break her phone.

"She's pretty upset," I whispered.

Sonya huffed. "Some people don't appreciate how lucky they are."

Jones stalked off. Jenna went back into her house, which was directly behind the trailer my friends had pointed out earlier.

Soon a woman dressed in black jeans and a red T-shirt approached. She had a giant megaphone and used it even though we stood all of two feet away.

"Will the new inflatable crowd please follow me?" she bellowed.

I raised my eyebrows at my friends.

Sonya shrugged. "At least she said 'please.'"

"Hold it! Stop right there!" the megaphone woman yelled, pointing to our group. "You look like minors."

"We are," Beatrix piped up. "But we have release forms." She collected all of ours and handed over the small stack.

The woman rifled through them, then had everyone walk to the corner of Prospect Park West.

As soon as we got there, Beatrix grabbed my arm and whispered, "Omigosh, that's Brandon Wilson!"

She pointed to a short guy stepping out of the trailer opposite Seth Ryan's.

"Who?" I asked.

"He was in Seth's last two movies. Remember?"

I squinted at the guy. His hair wasn't straight or curly, just puffy. And the color wasn't exactly red or brown, but somewhere in between. He seemed pretty pale, at least from far away. I tried to picture him in a vampire costume. Then dressed as a dog. "Oh, yeah," I said. "How cool!"

"Think we should ask for his autograph?" asked Lucy.

"No way," said my brother.

We watched Brandon talk to Jones and then head back into his trailer.

Then we saw Jones check with Zander on the progress of the snowmen.

Next we watched someone come around and adjust a bunch of lights. I figured they'd need us to do something sometime soon, but everyone ignored us for the next thirty minutes.

"Being an extra involves a lot of standing around," I said to Lucy as someone finally came over and asked us to cross the street. Then we had to stand around there while a group of props people, led by Zander, built new and better snowmen.

Finally, twenty minutes later, Jones barked at us through a megaphone. "Extras—please walk to the end of the block and mill around inconspicuously."

"I don't do a lot of milling," I whispered. "I think I'm going to be conspicuous."

"Shh!" said Beatrix.

We all shuffled over. It's hard to walk in a big crowd, and harder to act natural when you know there are cameras rolling. "Okay, got it. Now go back to where you started and do it again," Jones said. "This time with more feeling."

After doing this same thing six more times, I started worrying about my dogs. They had to be dying to go out. Maybe volunteering to be an extra had been a giant mistake.

I had a lot of homework tonight, too. Not to mention a history test tomorrow, and twenty pages still to read about the Trail of Tears. I didn't know if we'd been standing around for a long time or if it just seemed like that because I was so bored.

I checked my watch. Yup—it had been a long time.

Suddenly, Jones yelled into his megaphone again.

"You! In the green hoodie!" I looked down at my sweatshirt. It was green. I looked around. No one else in the crowd wore a green hoodie. He'd singled me out. But why? I had this feeling like I'd just failed a big test, and the most important information on it was *don't talk*.

But now it was too late. Jones Reynaldo stopped right in front of me.

"Will you stop checking your watch? You're ruining this entire scene. Now we have to shoot all over again."

"I'm so sorry," I said. "It's just—is this going to take much longer?"

"Yes!" he said. "Now get back to your place and stop looking so bored."

I moved back to where I'd been standing, but I could only follow half of his instructions because I'm just not that good of an actor. "Well, um, how much longer?" I asked. I didn't mean to be rude, but I had to know. There were dogs depending on me!

Jones turned around and glared at me. His entire face turned red as he lowered his megaphone and approached. "Who are you?" he asked.

"I'm Maggie Brooklyn Sinclair. It's nice to meet you." I held out my hand. He stared at it like I'd offered him up a rotten fish.

"You think I care?" he huffed.

"Well, you did ask." I put my hands in my sweatshirt pockets. I didn't like this guy.

Now that he stood so close, I saw he had a few pieces

of straw stuck in his hair. Anyone else, I would've told them about it. But Jones? I was afraid to say anything. The guy was seriously angry, and I was seriously intimidated.

"All I meant was, who are you to be interrupting my shoot?"

"Oh," I said. "I guess I'm an extra. But when I signed up I didn't think it would take this long. I only have so much extra time. Ha ha . . . And I'm sort of, well, out of it."

"What are you saying?" he asked.

"That I have to go."

"What?"

I wondered if he was hard of hearing. Maybe I should ask to borrow his megaphone?

"I have to—" I started to repeat myself, speaking louder this time, but he interrupted.

"You can't leave. I'm not finished with my scene. And no one walks off a Jones Reynaldo set."

"But I really have to go."

"Then I'm throwing you off! Quit wasting my time! Get out of here!"

"I'm so sorry," I said, with all sincerity. Yes, this guy was rude; yes, he was a bully, but I didn't want to mess up his movie. I tried to explain. "If I'd known how long this would take when we started, I never would've—"

"Why are you still talking?" he screamed, grabbing his hair. "I said leave. I never want to see you again. Just vanish."

I giggled. I just couldn't help it.

"What's so funny?" he asked.

"You said 'vanish,'" I said. "And your movie is called *Vanished*—right?"

"Right," he said slowly, not quite believing.

"So it's funny, is all."

Jones stared at me like he wanted to strangle me.

Then he threw his clipboard on the ground and stomped on it, reminding me of the last time Beckett's moms told him he couldn't have any more cookies.

Throwing a tantrum over a cookie I could relate to. Especially since one of his moms is such an awesome baker—a pastry chef at one of my and Finn's favorite restaurants. (One that, incidentally, does not serve brunch.)

But this? I didn't know what else to say.

Jones screamed, "You'll never work in this town again!"

This made no sense whatsoever, but it kind of freaked me out. And sometimes when I'm nervous or confused I can't help but laugh.

Unfortunately, this seemed to be one of those times.

I felt the laughter bubble deep in my stomach. It

traveled up into my throat; I couldn't help it. And then it came out.

Yup. I laughed. In Jones Reynaldo's face. Seeing him so irate with all that straw in his hair? The contrast was too much; it just made me laugh harder.

"What's so funny?" he asked.

I tried to explain myself between fits of giggles, but it wasn't easy getting the words out. "Well, I'm actually going to work. You see, I'm a dog walker, and I—"

"I don't care!" he shouted, pulling at his hair with both hands. "Just get out of my face and don't come back. I never want to see you again!"

Well, the feeling was mutual, but I didn't say so. I turned to my friends and said good-bye. Lucy waved. Finn just shook his head—half embarrassed, half trying not to laugh himself.

Beatrix and Sonya backed away like they were afraid to be associated with me. Probably they were worried *they'd* get thrown off the set for just knowing me, and I didn't blame them. I knew how important this was to them, and I didn't want to stand in their way of seeing the amazing Seth Ryan.

If they got to see him, that is.

In truth, we'd been standing out in the fake snow and the real cold for over an hour, and all we'd seen was Jones Reynaldo. And that Brandon guy. And my parents' friend Jenna. And a scared props guy named Zander, and the megaphone lady, and a bunch of other crew members.

As I headed down the street, I noticed something out of the corner of my eye.

In the window of the trailer—the one with all the security guards—someone waved.

His face seemed so familiar. One I'd seen on TV and in movies and in every magazine there is. He was Seth Ryan.

Except the strange part was, he seemed to be waving at me.

"Hey?" I half asked as I waved back, figuring this must be some big misunderstanding. Like, maybe he was merely Seth Ryan's look-alike.

Except when he smiled at me, I knew for sure, because Seth Ryan's smile is unforgettable.

So, that was weird enough, but he seemed to be waving me over, too.

At least it looked that way. I glanced over my shoulder, figuring there must be someone behind me—Jones or another actor or someone else involved in the movie.

But no—this side of the street remained empty.

I turned back around. Not only was Seth still there, he'd also leaned out of his window. "Hey, can you come here for a second?" he asked.

"Sure." I moved closer. "You do mean—"

Except I didn't get to finish my sentence. Because before I knew it, someone grabbed me by the arm and yanked me away.

Leslie Margolis is the author of many books for young readers, including the Annabelle Unleashed series and the next Maggie Brooklyn Mystery, *Vanishing Acts*. She lives with her family in Brooklyn, New York, in a neighborhood filled with mysteries, dogs, and even some mysterious dogs. Please visit her online at www.lesliemargolis.com.